Baby's First Felony

Books by John Straley

Baby's
First
Felony

JOHN STRALEY

Published by Soho Press in 2018
Soho Press, Inc.
853 Broadway
New York, NY 10003

Library of Congress Cataloging-in-Publication Data

Straley, John, 1953– author.
Baby's first felony / John Straley.
Series: A Cecil Younger investigation ; 7
I. Title
PS3569.T687 B33 2018 813'.54—dc23 2017055195

ISBN 978-1-61695-878-7
eISBN 978-1-61695-879-4

Interior art (pages 245–251) by Doug Comstock.

Printed in the United States

10 9 8 7 6 5 4 3 2 1

This book is dedicated to all the public defenders, and their clients. No matter how hard their circumstances, no matter how bad the facts or the prejudice against them, they stand up in court every day and assert their right to tell their unique, complex story. Without good lawyers, the poor and the neglected would be in jail already. They deserve more respect than I showed them here.

To me clowns aren't funny. In fact, they're kinda scary. I've wondered where this started and I think it goes back to the time I went to the circus and a clown killed my dad.

—Jack Handy

Our torments also may, in length of time, Become our Elements.

—John Milton, *Paradise Lost*

PART ONE:
The Allocution

If it please the Court: Your Honors, I stand before you today to tell the story of what happened. My words are not to be offered as any form of excuse, not even as an explanation, but I want to tell you the entire experience as it happened to me. Then, of course, you will be free to decide what you will.

It was the year of a hundred and six consecutive days of rain, and I had lost my daughter to her cell phone. The rain began at the end of summer, but the days were indistinguishable from late fall, each one blending to another in a slurry of rainfall, brightened only by a sunbreak a few minutes each day. The first completely dry day did not occur until December, when we had a cold high-pressure system move in that brought freezing temperatures that turned Swan Lake into a mirror of ice.

People's moods in Sitka, Alaska, were irritable both during and after the rain. This story starts in September before the darkest of the dark days had hit. This was still during the period of the jokes and well before the deaths and mayhem.

Todd had been asking me about the meaning of the Buddhist concept of "right relationship." Now, Your Honors, I know you might think I'm already beginning to drift, but bear with me, for this turns out to be one of the more slippery of the foundational stones of the eight-fold path—not that there are any real bodhisattvas in this cast of characters. But there are, as they say, many ways to get lost in this world, and "wrong relationship" is one of the most common.

As you may remember from the previous briefing, Todd lives in my house and has for many years. He was involved in the circumstances of this crime, a fact that I still regret. He and I are both now in our late fifties, and we relate to each other as brothers, even though there was a time when he was my ward, and I essentially had legal custody of him after his parents passed away. Todd rests comfortably on the solidly affected end of the Asperger's scale. Recently he has been learning to tell jokes as part of his occupational therapy. Joke telling, it turns out, helps create a kind of ready-made emotional relationship for people with autism. They say funny things, people laugh, display emotion and the autistic person laughs in response to the other person's laughter and presto: without having a clue of what an inner emotional world is like, they have entered into an emotional relationship.

Todd has lived his life with a series of obsessions. He has been fascinated with the patterns on manhole covers and the mechanics of how whales swim across the ocean. He has memorized the populations of all the major cities in the world and knows the make and model of almost every audio recording device ever manufactured. He loves animals and children, and his current interests include Buddhism and telling jokes.

Todd and I were walking back from work. I had walked from the Public Defender Agency, where I worked as a criminal defense investigator. I had stopped off at the jail to see one of our clients who had been locked up, and then I went over to the senior center to pick up Todd from his job in the kitchen. The rain was easing up to a light pebbling on the lake, and a few ducks were waddling in the middle of the street where someone had dumped a full bag of chips out of their car. This was irritating to the drivers along Lake Street but not enough for anyone to blow their horn, because it appeared that most everyone still enjoyed watching the ducks.

"Cecil, what is a right relationship?" Todd asked.

I took a deep breath. I was in a kind of peevish mood. The man I had just seen in jail was someone I had known for years who had stolen glassware out of a chemistry lab. He was found curled up in the gym where he had passed out after drinking the pure grain alcohol he had run across in the lab. He had fallen on the beakers several times as he made his way to the gym, so the linoleum floor was smeared red with blood, and his clothes sparkled like sequins when two cops and a dispatcher hoisted him into the booking area. This would be the first time he would be tried as an adult for burglary. His father was dead from walking drunk off a dock, and he had broken his mother's heart so many times she had tough-loved him out of the house as a life-saving measure. I don't like to use real names for anyone not named as a co-defendant, so I call him Sweeper, like the clown who sweeps up the spotlight. He is hard to help.

"I don't know, Todd. I don't know what a right relationship is."

"Don't you and Jane Marie have a right relationship?"

"Well . . . Yeah . . . I think so . . . I used to think so. But nothing is perfect."

"It's 'right.' Not 'perfect,'" Todd said as we walked. He is bald now. His glasses are his only hairline. Still he walks with a tottering flat-footed walk of a trained bear.

What irritated me about trying to explain religious concepts to Todd was that I wanted to tell him the truth, even though he would have no idea if I was being accurate and would take it on good faith. This bothers me.

"There is an old story about a man the Gods doomed to push a rock up a mountain. Remember that one?"

"Sisyphus," Todd said. He had gone through a long Greek and Roman obsession. "Yes."

"I think, we are all like that, buddy. Life is like that. Pushing that rock up the hill. What you are looking for is the person who understands your particular punishment, a person who will not pester you about rolling the rock up the hill. If you are lucky you find a person to kiss the bleeding callouses on your hands, and one for whom you will do the same."

"Oh." He stopped and looked at me. The raindrops on his glasses trembled as if they were Christmas ornaments swinging behind the windows of his thick lenses. Finally, a man in a pickup truck honked his horn, and the ducks scattered in a squall of feathers. Todd had a quizzical look on his face, and I could tell he was running the whole idea of sharing God's punishment through his mind like a vending machine trying to process a well-made slug.

"Tell me your joke today," I said.

Jane Marie, my wife, had been keeping on me to vet the jokes Todd was learning, for since it was known that Todd was telling jokes, people all over town were happy to tell him new ones, and Jane Marie worried some were not appropriate for all audiences and Todd would get himself in trouble. There had been an incident a few years ago when a little girl was crying outside the swimming pool, and she asked Todd if he could take her in to help her change into her suit, and he said he couldn't and that he was sorry, and when the little girl asked why, Todd explained that the locker room was for women only because, "Vaginas were generally considered private and were only really comfortable being exposed to other females in situations such as locker rooms or some public restrooms." Well, the lifeguard on duty heard the last of this, and there was a small-town kerfuffle about his choice of language, and Todd couldn't go to the swimming pool without me for a while, and it caused Jane Marie some heartburn in the joke department.

Todd took a deep breath and straightened his glasses. "A little boy was sitting on the curb in town eating a big handful of chocolate bars, one after another, and an old man comes up to him and says, 'You know, young man, you really shouldn't eat so much chocolate. It's not good for you,' and the little boy says, 'I don't know, my grandpa lived to be one hundred and three.' The old man said, 'Oh, I'm sorry, did your grandpa eat a lot of chocolate?' and the little boy said, 'No but he learned to mind his own fucking business.'"

By this time, we were through the roundabout and to the only stoplight downtown, and the wind was hitting us straight on without obstruction from the east. Todd's glasses were now a haze of mist, dotted with raindrops. Though we could have crossed without danger to get undercover on the opposite corner, we waited in the soaking wind because Todd honors all laws.

"It's a good joke," I said. "If you tell it with anyone under twelve years old around, just change the 'fuck' to 'damn.' You'll be fine."

Todd nodded. He had taken many similar notes and understood the F-word problem.

"Cecil?" he asked.

"What?" I responded.

"Why was the little boy eating chocolate bars sitting on the curb of the street?"

The light changed but just before we stepped down off the curb I considered his question. I never like to brush him off or give him the impression I'm not giving his inquiries full consideration.

"It's just funnier. I guess." We hurried across the street.

By the time we got home the house was in a full frenzy of pre-dinner homework bickering: Jane Marie was stirring a pot of boiling red sauce, and Blossom was standing at the head of a bare table staring into her phone.

"Cecil, will you talk to your daughter?" was my wife's greeting as I topped the stairs to our living room/kitchen, which looked out over the channel. Blossom did not acknowledge my existence.

"Mi familia!" I said as happily as I could. "Daughter, is there trouble in paradise?"

"Mom is being a bitch," Blossom said, without raising her heavily mascaraed eyes from her phone, which she appeared to be drumming with her thumbs.

Jane Marie slapped the spoon into the sauce and started to make a move around the stove like a professional wrestler about to climb the turnbuckle to go for a body slam.

"Now hold on . . . everyone. Hold on." I moved in front of Jane Marie to gather her up in my arms. "You *are* such a bitch. I knew that the first time I met you." I kissed her on the lips.

"She can't call me that, Cecil." Jane Marie's eyes

were tired and sad, but every muscle in her body was coiled. She was ready to break.

"Listen," I said, "let me set the table. Blossom, would you please pick some dinner music that will not cause us to slit our wrists, and could we have a meal that does not involve having the police called?" Blossom grunted and sat down and started scrolling through her music.

"You are such a tool," she muttered.

"Thank you sweetheart," I said.

The advantage of asking Blossom to provide the music for dinner was she had to place her phone in a cradle beside the stereo system. She chose the Mountain Goats album *All Hail West Texas* because she knew I had once said that I liked it, but she set the volume far too high, knowing it would irritate the shit out of her mother, particularly the chorus of "Hail Satan!" in the first song. Jane Marie sat gritting her teeth as I scooped the sauce onto her plate, and I signaled Todd to turn down the volume.

To give a little more background to the tension in our family, about nine months ago a girl from the high school had dropped out and then gone missing. Her name was Melissa Bean. She had twin baby girls. We had known her and had helped her with her children. We still took care of the babies when the grandparents were overwhelmed. Melissa had fallen away in the last few months before her disappearance. She had been sullen and quiet, angry most of the time. "Drugs," her parents said. She was never home; then there were new friends and strange calls.

She was always tired, seemed scared of something but got snappy if you asked her about it. Her mom was worried that her daughter was growing so thin. Finally, after the Permanent Fund checks, our oil money payments, came out she was gone. No rumors. No body. It was a nightmare for Jane Marie and the many mothers of sullen teenage girls.

I was worried about Blossom as well, but I always worried. I'm now a fifty-six-year-old father of a teenager. I'm always tired too. I don't see any of the obvious signs of drug use. Blossom is smart and bookish. She reads a lot. She makes films with her phone. She stays up late watching movies and talking to her nerdy friends. She likes to argue and cares passionately about the things she likes. The druggy people I knew—and I knew a lot of them—didn't give a whit about John Darnielle, or whether he sounded better solo or with his band, or if the whole "lo-fi" phenomenon was bullshit or not, but for some reason Blossom did. Now, is she in danger of becoming a pretentious thirteen-year-old hipster? Probably, but Your Honors, cut me some parental slack here. This is Sitka, Alaska, and being a tad pretentious or being a lot pretentious when you are thirteen is a far cry from being a meth head swallowed up by the drug underworld, and preferable to that as well.

But Jane Marie worried about it, night and day, particularly since Blossom's dear little playmate Emily dyed her hair blue and, in a twist on her best friend's name, changed her own name to Thistle.

"Cecil, can Thistle spend the night tomorrow?" Calling us by our first names was another new development that drove Jane Marie crazy.

"It's fine with me." I looked at Jane Marie and she nodded down at her food. "Is it okay with her mom?"

"Ah . . . she doesn't live with her mom anymore. She lives someplace else, with another family, I think."

"What?" Jane Marie put down her fork. "Honey, what happened with Emily?"

"I don't know. She just moved out. It happens." Now they were both looking at their food.

Todd asked for some more spaghetti, and I dished him some in silence.

"Blossom . . ." Jane Marie's voice was starting to crack, "when did this happen?"

"I dunno."

"Jesus Christ," Jane Marie said softly and a tear traced down her cheek.

"Why are you mad at me? I didn't do anything," Blossom said.

"No one said you did, honeybunny," I said.

"I'm sorry," Jane Marie said. She got up from the table and put her half-full plate of crab pasta in the sink and walked back into the office. John Darnielle and the Mountain Goats were singing "Color in Your Cheeks" as Todd asked if he could have another piece of French bread, and I told him he could.

Your Honors, you know from the previous briefing that I have a criminal history. You know that I am an alcoholic. At the time of this incident I had not had a drink in twenty years. All of my earlier offenses, the offenses that caused me to lose my driving privileges and tarnish my record were all alcohol related. What you may not know is that I was also a child of alcoholics, though my parents were not as extreme or as dramatic in their drinking as I turned out to be. But as a child of alcoholics, I grew up with a need to please, and a need to try and to set the chaos right, to sweep up the broken glass and smooth over the arguments. Some have suggested that was the reason I became a criminal defense investigator. I don't know about that, but I'm sure it helped when it came to being the father of a teenager.

So I knocked on Blossom's door later and when I didn't hear anything, I said her name. It wasn't until I heard her small voice say, "Come in," that I opened the door. Her room was tiny, not much more than a closet really; it only had room for a bed and a chair and a dresser, but it had a window that looked over the commercial channel of Sitka's harbor. Below, the water slapped against our boat launch at high tide. The gulls mewed almost all night every season of the year, and even in the rain they sat in the calm water like bars of soap.

"Why does she hate me so much, Cecil?"

"She doesn't hate you, baby. You worry her, that thing with Melissa scares her so much."

"I don't do drugs. She knows that. I want to be on the debate team, and you can't be on the debate team if you smoke pot. Maybe after that . . . you know . . ."

"Okay, fair enough," I brushed back her hair. She had washed her face. There was none of the badly applied makeup or the mascara. There, once again, was the girl I knew. "Look at me, sweetie," I said softly. She lifted her head. "Do you love her still?"

She looked down at her quilt, which had whales and birds woven into the fabric. I looked around the high ceilings of her room at her childhood mobiles, which had been a gift from her mom. On the walls were the pictures of research trips, shots of Blossom photographing whales out at sea, and one of her shooting a crossbow to collect DNA samples from killer whales. Her shelves sagged with glass balls we had found on the sandy beaches offshore.

"Sure . . . sure I love her. She's my mom, but she's not fair to me all the time."

"Ah baby . . . that is the truth and probably the source of all great music."

Blossom squinched up her teenaged face in recognition of some more adult "wait till you're older" bullshit.

"When Thistle comes over, can I talk with her? I want to find out what's happening with her family," I said.

"Don't interview her, Cecil, and don't give her any crap about where she's staying okay?"

"B, can you for a second not talk to me like you are a cop? I'm your father for Pete's sake. I've known her a long time, and I want to help her, okay?"

"Yes, Cecil."

"Good night, honey pie." I kissed my only daughter, then turned out the light, as the gulls rose on soft white feathers, some of them settling on our roof for the night.

The next morning the rain was a quiet patter on the roof, building to a steady staccato as it gathered strength. I was the first one up and could enjoy a half hour of quiet: the hum of the furnace on its morning setting and the rumble of the teapot warming up. A few boats headed out to clean up their catches for the year. I sat at the table in my robe and read the thin paper from the night before with my feet on the heat register. There was an article about Melissa Bean and how the reward for information leading to her "recovery" had been increased to twenty thousand dollars. I noticed it no longer was posted for her "return." I had heard they were considering holding an inquest, perhaps the family wanted an end to it and to have something final to tell their young toddlers.

An eagle soared lazily over the channel and the teapot whistled. The rest of the household stirred, and we ate our breakfast, then performed our morning ablutions—last-minute homework, lunch packing, coat finding, and permission-slip signing—and were out the door for our walk. I made the circuit with Blossom and Todd, dropping each one off, not that I really needed to. I mostly just enjoyed it, even though it irritated B. Blossom adored Todd, and for some inexplicable reason thought he was unbelievably cool, but I was clearly not.

We hit the sidewalk in front of the green house on Katlian Street with the planter boxes on the second floor, and headed north past the cold storage. Usually I fall into my own rhythm quickly, but this morning Blossom did not have here ear buds in, and she was showing Todd what was on her phone screen. I could hear Todd's recorded voice, flat and unaffected: "A cowboy walks into a bar, looks up, and there are three signs, hamburgers: five dollars, cheeseburgers: six dollars, and hand jobs: ten dollars. So, he looks around . . ."

"Wait a minute," I stopped them. "What is that?"

"It's Todd telling a joke. It's great. I filmed it. It's already got two thousand hits, and it's been up less than twelve hours!"

"You posted it online?"

"Duh . . . Of course. It's epic."

I had ringing in my ears. I had heard the expression "seeing red" before, but this was the first time that I think I was actually experiencing it. Todd stood there looking at me with his blank goofy smile.

"It's epic," he said.

"Did you consider? Did you consider Todd? Did you think that you might be exploiting Todd's . . . Todd's personality?"

"God, Cecil . . . what a snob. I asked him. It's okay with you isn't it, Todd?"

"I had better get to work," was all he said, and he walked quickly up the sidewalk and through the rain that was picking up now and bouncing off his yellow slicker.

"I did. I did ask him, and he said yes!" Blossom yelled.

"I know, but you know that he would do anything you said, just about. He trusts you. That's what makes this so creepy, B. Can't you see that?"

"It's a funny joke. It's not that bad, and the way he tells it is super funny."

"B, it's hurtful. People only think it is funny because of Todd's condition."

"I know for a fact it doesn't hurt Todd. You know I wouldn't do anything to hurt him."

"Okay . . . just please take it down. Are there any more like it?"

"Maybe . . . a few."

"Maybe how many?"

"Maybe a dozen . . . or two."

"Ho . . . ly . . . crap. Don't breathe a word of this to your mother. We are going to have to have a damage control strategy session if this comes out. And please, please, please . . . take them down."

"All of them?" she whined.

"Jesus Christ! Look at my face, listen to my voice. Am I acting serious?"

"Yes . . ."

"Okay then take down all the footage you have of Todd that is available to anyone outside of our immediate family. What should be private will be private once again by dinnertime tonight, is that understood? If not, I will have to think up some unpleasant punishment, which I hate, hate, hate to do because it involves me acting like a cop, which is my least favorite thing to do in the world."

"Yeah because you suck at it."

"Bad time for sarcasm, little girl. Now go to school and don't curse and make us proud."

"Yes, Cecil."

We had been walking the entire time we had been arguing, and we ended up at the cutoff by the gas station for the middle school. I took her cell phone from her, and she padded off up the hill to the back of the school with her backpack humped up on her tiny shoulders.

When I climbed the stairs to work, our office manager, Rhonda, was standing by her desk with Gus, the office hound, who was balancing a dog biscuit on his nose.

"Watch this."

I sat down next to Marvin Pete, an obese Native man in a Seattle Seahawks number twelve jersey, and watched as Gus balanced the treat on his nose for several seconds until Rhonda said, "Pop it," and Gus bounced the treat in the air and snapped it up in his jaws.

"Good boy!" she cooed and lavished him with kisses. Rhonda is a glamorous Tlingit woman with a nice wardrobe and an athletic body.

"Dogs," Marvin murmured to me, "dogs have all the luck."

"They enjoy a right relationship, Marvin." I smiled at him. "Are you here to see David? Does he know you are here?"

Marvin shrugged his shoulders with his eyes still on Rhonda. "Who knows with that guy."

At that moment David Ryder came out of the back office wearing his usual rumpled, pleated khakis and a stained button-down shirt. David is an African American man in his midforties. A dedicated public defender originally from outside Washington, DC, he took a fishing trip fifteen years ago and fell in love with the place. He and his daughter, Rochelle, and a local cab driver named Hank Moore, make up the backbone of what the Democrats in town refer to as Sitka's "black community."

"Mr. Pete, I'm glad you are here, I will be with you in just a second. I need to talk with Cecil in his office for a moment." He pointed at my door.

My office was in fact a break room, copying center, conference room and storage unit for our three-person operation. There were no windows and the configuration had been changed around so often that there were two doorknobs that stuck through the outside walls in seemingly random spots. I settled behind my desk, and David closed my door, picked up my baseball mitt and ball and sprawled in the overstuffed chair and started throwing the ball over his head and catching it in the glove.

"Jesus, Cecil . . . what are these people thinking?"

"Ah . . . thinking?"

"I mean Sweeper. You talked to him, right?"

"Yes . . . I stopped by yesterday. I gave him the basics. What is the problem?"

"He wants to seek employment with the city."

"Seeking employment with the city" was our term for wanting to become a snitch, usually in hopes of consideration on current charges. Sweeper was in on burglary of the school, maybe a probation violation. He had been caught stealing glassware, beakers, and of all things, protective aprons from the science lab, and of course the liter of grain alcohol.

"Really?" I asked, not very helpfully. "Not to insult the Sweeper, but he doesn't strike me as trustworthy enough for a position with the police. What is he looking at here?"

"Well, that's the thing," David was almost prone in the chair now, throwing the hardball up toward the fluorescent lights. "The DAO says they are looking into adding some DV charges. Apparently he and Sherrie got into it again last night."

Sherrie Gault was the Sweeper's long-time dance partner. Sherrie had also been a client, but not for a few years. We had all been rooting for Sherrie to wise up and leave the Sweeper in the dust.

David caught the ball and slapped it into the webbing of his mitt. "Anyway, I want you to go to the hooscow and talk to him. Get a broad proffer of what he might know—you know the drill: no names, but would he be willing to wear a wire? That kind of thing. Warn him about what life is like for a snitch and tell him how insecure and slow the process is. I doubt the Sweeper has a get out of jail free card. Did you give him a copy of *Baby's First Felony?*"

Baby's First Felony was a self-help book that David Ryder was always working on. Intended for intellectually challenged criminals, it was based on firsthand experience we'd had with our clients. It was going to have a limited print run on laminated pages and thick wire binding. It would have helpful advice that David and I had learned over the years, such as: *When confessing to a murder, stay away from hunting analogies, such as: "I know I had to put him out of his misery, so I put him down clean."*

Also: *In any statement to the police, be sure to avoid the phrase, "Just how stupid do you think I am?"* And: *Don't wear the tennis shoes you stole to court when the guy you stole them from will be there to testify and his name is still written inside of them.* These are bits of advice we had learned the hard way.

"Okay. I will head right over."

David paused a second, and I could tell he was holding something back.

"What?" I asked him.

"If he wants to talk about bail, ask about Wynn Sanders. The guy gives me the creeps, but he has put up bail for Sweeper. See if Sweeper wants to get involved with Sanders again."

Wynn Sanders was a local Libertarian/Republican owner of some businesses around town, including a large hotel. He had come from Oklahoma some thirty years before and wore a short-brimmed Stetson hat, one of the few in town. He also chewed on unlit cigars, or maybe that was a just detail my memory invented to fit my current recollection of him as some kind of an

unrepentant southern cross-burning racist. Sanders
had actually been on the city assembly. He was a local
Republican booster of from-the-ground-up capital-
ism. He was of the opinion that the government had
no place in the lives of its citizens, and sometimes he
helped people with their bail money. He was a good
citizen. He had helped both the Sweeper and Sherrie.
He clearly had a complex and bitter relationship with
the criminal justice system. He hated David, but he
supported many of our clients.

"Why's he give you the creeps?" I asked.

"Oh . . . you know . . . the usual." He continued to
catch fly balls in his imagination.

"You think he's racist?" I held my hand up and my
boss chucked it to me.

"You mean a hood-wearing, cross-burning kind of
guy?"

"Yeah, I guess. Did Sanders say something to you?"
I threw the ball back.

"It's one thing to hate me for my job. I get that. He
had a bad roll when his daughter died, but there is a
very angry vibe about him. I guess I just don't like his
manners."

David had used this expression before. "Not liking
someone's manners" was his own way of expressing
that he suspected a person of having a racist attitude,
or more accurately, a more racist attitude than the
common underlying radiation of racism that exists in
Alaska, every second of every day.

Sanders's daughter had been a client. She had

been caught selling heroin to an undercover cop. She "sought city employment" and plead guilty to a reduced charge of possession, down from distribution and misconduct with a weapon. When the cops frisked her outside the bar they found one of her daddy's many pistols. The deal was completely her choice. She had been caught, the evidence was going to stand, and junkies when first arrested, hate . . . hate, the idea of doing any time at all, particularly entitled white girls who essentially don't see what all the fuss is about.

She did her service for the city and about ninety days in jail, but three months after she got out of rehab she died of a "relapse overdose," which is when a junky has been craving heroin for so long that they give in and binge, thinking that they can take right back up where they left off with the same dose, but with a clean system, that shot kills them.

Wynn Sanders took the entire thing out on David, insisting that her original possession and sale was a youthful experiment, and the deal she took put her in the drug world and caused his little girl to become a junky. In Wynn Sanders's mind, her public defender had killed her.

I knew what David meant. Sanders had a taut, bloodless vibe. He looked a bit like an angry secretary of defense during war time: he had wire-rim glasses and a buzz cut; the skin on his temples seemed paper thin. His mouth was like a crack in an egg. Even without the hat or the cigar he seemed to vibrate with the hostility of an affronted southern sheriff whenever we were around. There is nothing quite like the rage of a wealthy white man when his privilege is not respected.

David Ryder caught the ball and turned back to me. "Anyway, I have heard from Sweeper that Sanders has offered to put up bail for both Sherrie and Sweep, so inquire about that. Then when you get back, I want you to talk with Mr. Pete. We need to help him get into treatment."

"Sure, boss."

Baby's First Felony has an entire chapter on talking to the police, which could be boiled down to: *Don't do it. Don't ever do it. And don't ever do it.* Which makes becoming a snitch one of the worst ideas ever. First, everyone hates snitches, your fellow criminals for one. Convicts hate snitches with a passion, but the cops are not too keen on them either when it comes right down to it, no matter what they say about "turning your life around" and "serving your community" and "getting a second chance." For most cops, once a bad guy always a bad guy . . . there are a few instances of them taking a frail little waif of a drug-addicted girl into their hearts, but that is pure sexism. Most snitches are forever orphans.

Another important piece of advice, besides not speaking pig latin to the girlfriend you are trying to talk into building a bomb over the prison phone, is to never use the prison phones in the first place. No matter how many times you are reminded that the calls are recorded. Somehow or another most of our clients think that either their calls have been exempted or that the cops cannot break codes such as ig-pay atin-lay, or their native Spanish tongue. Sweeper had not called in the two days he was in, so maybe he was heeding that advice.

Looking at Sweeper chained to the wall in the interview room later in the Sitka jail, I could not imagine the cops taking him into their bosom. He was rail thin and was missing some teeth since he had played football for the Sitka Wolves, some seven years ago. He had that pink-skin shine of a fresh jail shower, but he shivered like someone who was still burning off the meth.

"How are you, sir, you remember me? I work with David."

"Yeah. When's he coming to see me?"

"Soon. He sent me. I'm covered by the same protection of confidentiality. Anything you say to me can't be used against you in any way."

"I understand. I want the fuck out of here. Now." He was picking at his forearm. "I didn't want to talk to him on the phone. You sure this room is okay?"

"Yes. They monitor the video for our protection but not the audio, at least they are not supposed to, and if we caught them listening to our conversation we would have a good shot at having your case dismissed."

"After a fucking year in here."

"Maybe. You want to provide information to the police?"

He had a thin goatee and black hair and an intricate tattoo of a locomotive on his forearm. He motioned with his cuffed finger and his goatlike chin for me to come closer. I leaned in close enough for him to bite my ear off.

"I know who killed that fucking girl, what's her name . . . Bean."

His breath smelled like peppermint toothpaste. I leaned back and looked at him. He waggled his eyebrows and grinned a gap-toothed smile. Proud of himself. Superior.

"You know she is dead."

There is also a section in *Baby's First Felony* about trying to make deals, such as trying to mitigate a burglary by admitting to a murder is not all that wise. This is called trading up.

"Bled out, cut up in pieces, and dumped overboard in the Sound," he said with the slightest bit of a grin.

"What you got for proof?"

"I can take them to where they butchered her up. Sure they cleaned, but shit, there is always something left. The cops can even just say they found something, and the pussy will talk."

"Why do this, now? Why not before?"

"I'm in jail. I want out."

"We've heard there may be domestic violence charges coming against you from Sherrie. Is that true?"

"She won't testify." Those words fell like stones in mud. "I want out now. Let's do this."

"What about bail?"

"I won't need bail once they learn what I know."

"You want me to call Mr. Sanders?" I said referring to the man with the possible bail money.

"Fuck Mr. Sanders."

This was fine by me, but I warned him not to talk to the cops until he heard back from me. I promised that he would hear from us by the end of today. I told him that there was no such thing as a get out of jail free card, and life as a snitch, particularly for snitching out a brutal murder, had its own consequences. He just stared at me. He was a scholar of the law now. Because he knew one thing I didn't know; he knew everything.

"Get hopping," he said. "I don't want to spend another night in here."

There is a section of *Baby's First Felony* entitled, "Reality Is More Complicated than Anyone Knows . . . and in Your Case . . . That's a Good Thing." It advises patience and listening to your attorney. It was clear that the Sweeper had not, and would not read this section. He was smart. Oh, yes, he was.

The rain was falling hard now and droplets were jumping in the brown water of the gutters. I stopped to buy Rhonda and David some coffee and myself some tea. I tried to scrub the image of small fish swimming in and out of Melissa Bean's eye sockets from my mind.

I had known the Sweeper's girlfriend, Sherrie Gault, from years ago. As a teenager her name just showed up in police reports. She was on the periphery of lots of hijinks: underage drinking and small break-ins. Soon enough she graduated to a client and a witness to major felonies: drugs and serious assaults. She had been charged with assaulting her baby son.

She swore she couldn't remember hitting him, and I
believed her. She had a crooked jaw, yet she was very
lovely; she wore a faux emerald earring, and her black
hair was the night around her face. On one of her
early morning visits to the office, I mentioned that she
looked nice, and her expression of disgust created a
hole in which I caught a glimpse of her . . . it was more
than disgust; after my compliment she looked at me
with pure loathing: loathing for me, who was obviously
lying, loathing for herself and her appearance and
hatred of the words that were trying to reach her. She
was a woman who could take a compliment only from
the Devil himself.

I asked if she had ever had any problems as a child
herself. At first she said, "No more than any other
kid." But when I took her through it step-by-step and
unpacked what she meant by "normal discipline," and
we got closer to what a babysitter had done to her, it
turned out that from age six to thirteen she had been
beaten on a daily basis to the point of heavy bruising
and unconsciousness. She started to cry, and she said
that she loved her baby, but she didn't know how to
discipline him when he cried. All her boyfriends, all
her lovers had been abusive. She had been to court-
ordered programs. She had been to drug and alcohol
programs. But words did not reach her, only pain, and
she could take a lot of it.

Back at the office, clients were sitting and standing
in what served as a waiting area. David was talking to
them in shifts and trying to write a motion that was

due at four-thirty that afternoon. I spoke with the ones I could. Most of them just wanted an update on what was happening with their case, some wanted to review their evidence, which was never very much fun for them. The police wore audio recorders and captured their words, and there were cameras in the booking section of the jail that usually caught just how drunk they had been. The night of their arrest was never a good night, and it usually drained the righteous indignation out of them. There were tears, some swearing, some redirection of blame. I had heard it all and let them vent, but it always came back to the law and what the evidence showed. Sometimes there was good news. Sometimes there were mistakes made by the police, sometimes terrible mistakes, resulting in an innocent person being arrested, but most of our caseload involved people who had become overwhelmed by the need to numb themselves with drugs or alcohol and had either driven a motor vehicle or hurt someone they loved.

Many of them had become, not friends exactly, but compatriots. The wayward, the desperate—we understood each other even across differences in race or gender. Though we never reveled in our past times together (for who really wants to relive their last arrest), we nodded to each other on the street and accepted that we had been through that shit together.

There had been many clowns: the sad ones and the manic ones. There was the Sad Clown, who drank until the point of blackout every day; and the Mute Clown, who had done a long jag for sexual assault of a minor, where the girl recanted and admitted that she had lied to help her mother in the divorce . . . twelve years into his sentence. There was the Gingerbread Man, who always ran away from the police when approached, whether on foot or in a car or on a four-wheeler. There might be some who can succeed at this, but we live on an island with seventeen miles of main road. There is the Tracer, who has such bad OCD that he must place his feet in his own footprints wherever he walks. He once spent two hours standing in the rain waiting for someone to come move a car out of the road where he had traveled earlier in the morning. I asked him once what it felt like if he didn't retrace his steps, and he said, "It feels as if I am no longer the same human being. If I walk around that car, the man on the other side, the wrong side of that car, is a phantom, and I am permanently stuck on the other side."

It wasn't until late in the afternoon that I was able to speak to David about the Sweeper's desire to work for the city. He nodded and listened quietly.

"Do you think he actually knows anything?" he asked when I finished.

"He acted like he did. He said he could lead them to the butcher shop. He said there would be evidence there, which sounds like something only a confident person would offer up."

"Well he's not a top priority right now, unless he calls again or comes in."

"Why is that?" I looked at my watch and saw that the

end of the workday was drawing near, and I was going to have to go back to the jail to keep my promise to Sweeper.

David was already looking through his motion and handing it off to Rhonda to get it to the court for filing as he spoke to me. "Sweeper is out of jail. The DAO did not file the domestic violence charges and they reduced his bail and cut him loose this afternoon."

"Just like that?"

"Yep. Forget about him. In fact, they picked up Sherrie. They are holding her on DV charges. She will be arraigned tomorrow. We will probably represent her because we didn't learn any confidential stuff from Sweeper, but we'll see. He didn't tell you much about it, did he?"

"Only that she wouldn't testify."

"It will probably be okay. Don't let him think you are working for him anymore. Let him know we are with Sherrie now, and find out what she has been up to lately, okay? Last I knew she was working in the card game and might be caught up in meth. Sad girl. DAO will want her in treatment probably to get her away from Sweeper. Talk to her tomorrow, Cecil, see if there is a new life out there for her."

Not exactly *Hawaii Five-0*, this job. My other clients were endurance champions of pain and dysfunction. During the day I had dealt with other charter members of *Baby's First Felony*'s Hall of Fame. Binky had been through treatment twelve times and his family had given up on him. He was in a tent in the rain. I

gave him food coupons that he traded for booze. He
was issued trespass orders from all the liquor stores
and now he had shoplifted mouthwash. He was dying.
But he still had the sweet face I recognized from when
I was a kid. He had been tough-loved by everyone else,
and I could see why, but I just couldn't bear to watch
him die.

The Fireman was always good for a changeup
because he wasn't a drinker. He was a conspiracy theo-
rist and a low-level burglar with a pain pill addiction
that had not yet blossomed into a heroin addiction.
He was a frequent DUI client and apparently loved the
feeling of walking into other people's houses: silent
. . . expectant. He was called the Fireman because if
the owner walked in on him, he would claim he had
smelled smoke and was there to help. He also loved
to come in with written works outlining his cultural
critiques, which ranged from anarcho-syndicalist to
vaguely Hunter S. Thompson–styled Libertarian talk
radio hooey. I welcomed him in, though David saw
him as a time suck. The Fireman had sent me four
faxes during the afternoon that were sitting on my
desk. I scanned them while I listened to my messages
and drank half a cup of coffee. The Fireman's large-
print messages were scrawled in black marker, which
added to their craziness. They always had tidbits of
information to add to the mounting government conspiracy against him. The first note read, *Patrol cars by
the house at 16:45 and 16:56. Nothing on the scanner. I had
a doctor's appointment at five . . . but canceled because of this*

surveillance. You need to tell David to file something with the court to stop this harassment.

The coffee was bitter by six o'clock, and I meant to ask Rhonda about it but I forgot. I put the Fireman's notes in his thick folder, sent a quick email to David passing on the request to file a motion to stop the police from driving on the Fireman's street and then I walked to the senior center to pick up Todd.

On weekends Todd will sometimes drink coffee at the Pioneer Bar in the early mornings. The Pioneer is a classic fisherman's bar and in the early morning, drinkers and nondrinkers alike gather. Once they understood that Todd was learning jokes they were more than happy to help him, which was the reason that Jane Marie wanted me to begin screening the jokes for appropriateness. I suspect that the joke that Blossom had selected to share with the world via the Internet had come from the Pioneer Bar. On the way home I asked Todd to tell it to me.

"Are you mad at me about this, Cecil?"

"Of course not. We just had a deal, remember? You were not supposed to tell any jokes to kids without you telling them to me first. Right?"

"I understand, Cecil. But B isn't a kid anymore, is she?"

"Is that what she tells you?"

"Yes. Repeatedly."

"Okay. Todd. Remember the prime directive in *Star Trek*?"

"Of course."

"Okay. Here is a new prime directive from me: Blossom is still a kid until you hear it from me that she isn't. Particularly when it comes to jokes and the Internet. Got it?"

"Yes."

"Okay . . . What's the joke?"

Todd straightens his glasses and continues walking in his singular flat-footed style. His voice is his usual uninflected monotone: "A cowboy walks into a bar, looks up and there are three signs: hamburgers: five dollars, cheeseburgers: six dollars, and hand jobs: ten dollars. So, he looks around and sees a very beautiful woman standing behind the counter of the establishment, and he walks up to her and asks, 'Excuse me, ma'am, but are you one of the ladies who gives the hand jobs?' and she says, 'I sure am, handsome, what can I do for you?' and the cowboy says, 'I was wondering if you could wash your hands because I would like a cheeseburger.'"

The rain was falling like BBs on our shoulders as we made our way past the Russian cathedral in the middle of town, and a raven sat perched on the lip of a black garbage can laughing at us as we passed.

"That is an excellent joke, Todd." I said. "I like it very much. Blossom is going to argue with me on this, I know, but I'm going to say it is not appropriate for a thirteen-year-old girl to be putting it up on the Internet. It is a close call."

"Really? Why?" Todd asked.

"Ah . . . Shit, Todd. We covered masturbation.

Nothing wrong with it and all. Hand jobs are when someone else does it to you. Not all that bad, but when you pay for it it's exploitative. Not that great."

"But the cowboy wants a cheeseburger."

"Exactly . . . which is what makes the joke funny, and this is why Blossom is going to be such a pain in the ass about it when I get home."

"Is she really a pain in the ass?" Todd sneaks a look at my ass and smiles. He loves metaphors.

"No. She is sweet, in a pain in the ass sort of way. She will be a fine woman—if she doesn't go to jail for killing her mother first."

It was Friday night and Thistle was our guest. When I walked up the stairs of our house, the door to Blossom's room was closed, and the sounds of the Screaming Females were blasting out a cover of a Taylor Swift song, and it sounded like the girls were jumping on Blossom's bed and screeching. Todd ducked into his room, and I went up to the kitchen.

Jane Marie sat at our big table, where there were papers scattered everywhere and her laptop was open.

"I have to get this grant application in, Cecil. I'm sorry. It has to be in tomorrow, and I can't hear myself think with that music. Can you make dinner?"

"Of course."

By the time the venison tacos were ready; the beans heated; the tomatoes, lettuce, and onions cut; cheese grated and tortillas warmed and waiting on the side bar, the grant application was tidied up in an acceptable draft for later work. Todd had cleared and set the table, and the girls were ready to come upstairs for their feeding ritual. They were both dressed in black knee-length dresses with lace collars and sleeves, looking vaguely like twins out of a Grant Wood painting. Blossom plopped in her seat without a word. Thistle sat and spoke up with a bright metallic braces smile.

"Hey ya, Mr. Younger. How's tricks?"

"Swell, T. How you doing?"

"Never better, thanks."

Jane Marie was putting away her computer. She fussed with her shirtsleeves. "Hi, Emily. How are you, honey? B says you aren't living at home, what's up?"

"Mom! Can you not interrogate her before we eat?" Blossom glared at her mother with a cold stare, and even though the child had gone through a major growth spurt in the last year and a half, she seemed to have shrunken down below the level of the table, perhaps out of spite for her parents' lack of coolness.

"Naw, that's okay, Ms. Y. My mom is going through a rough time with her new boyfriend. He is kind of a dick if you don't mind me saying so. He drinks a lot and he smacks her around and she won't call the police and if I try to call the police, they both say that they'll turn me over to social services or whatever, you know what I'm saying? It's a mess. My aunt says she is going to get her back into the program and going to meetings and everything, but I've got a good place to stay with some girls over at the apartments by the McDonald's. They are good people, and they take real good care of things. It's good. Really, it is."

Jane Marie handed her a plate with two warm tortillas with beans and meat on them, then a similar
plate to Blossom. She had a worried look on her face.
Thistle was skinny and her blue hair seemed comical
on her big, baby head. Blossom and I could tell Jane
Marie was about to wind up for a lecture. She took a
deep breath and said, "Honey, here's what I . . ."

"That sounds cool, Thistle . . ." I interrupted. "Who
are some of the other people in the apartment?"

"Just some girls. We pitch in on food and chores
and stuff. Each week we order a pizza. It's good, Mr.
Younger. My mom knows about it. It's cool." Thistle
wrapped up the plain meat and bean tortilla then
bit into it as fast as she could and smiled up at me
while she chewed. "Aw, the girls are all real cool, Mr.
Younger. It's no one you know. I'm certain. I don't
think any of them have ever been in trouble or nothing. Real goody two-shoes, you know. Prom queen
types. But, you know, they're not in school now."

"Got jobs then?" I handed her the sour cream and
salsa.

"Jobs? Heck, yea. We got jobs, and we go in together
on food and movies and stuff all the time."

"That's great. What kind of job did you get?"

"Cecil. Stop it man. You gonna get a big phone
book and start beating the answers out of her next?"
Blossom was picking the venison off of her taco.

"Naw . . . No sweat, B, I got me a job folding laundry
at the cleaners. It's cool."

I ate my taco and some salad, and we drank water

and some lemonade. Jane Marie made sure Thistle ate seconds, and we kept the girls at the table and talked about Jane Marie's grant application to study humpback whales that were feeding on salmon fry released by the hatcheries. Thistle showed some interest when Jane brought out her computer and showed videos of the whales surfacing right next to the hatchery pens. She sat up on her knees and leaned on her elbows, staring straight into the computer screen.

"Holy crap!" she said as a forty-foot whale surfaced next to the dock with its mouth fully open, engulfing thousands of gallons of water and unknown numbers of salmon fry.

The girls ate ice cream at the table with us, and we talked about music and movies. I asked Blossom if she had taken care of the chore we had discussed this morning. She nodded and said, "Almost," and I said, "I would like that completed by the time you go to bed please," and she nodded in agreement.

Jane Marie looked at me and then at Thistle, "Is this something I should know about?"

"Naw . . . we got this taken care of. It is something between us." I looked at Blossom. "Right?" and my little girl nodded in agreement.

Now, Your Honors, I want to mention this because it was the last "normal" night of my life, and there was nothing going through my mind but protecting my family and to some extent that little girl who was spending the night, which as you know I failed in doing. But that last night I was peaceful and happy, blissful in my ignorance. I sat on the couch with Jane Marie as she worked on her grant application, and I read a beautiful book by a colleague of hers named Eva Saulitas about her work and the killer whales in Resurrection Bay, and, Your Honors, I have to tell you that was the last time I remember feeling fully human. There for those few moments on that couch, reading that book and listening to the girls' music pounding in their room, watching the woman I loved do the work that mattered most to her. Now, as you know, all of that is gone.

Soon, it was late. I knocked on Blossom's door and waited for the music to go down before I knocked again and waited for her to ask me in. Blossom was in bed and Thistle was on a pad on the makeshift bunk that the desk could become. I asked Blossom about the videos of Todd, and she did not argue but simply said, "Yes," and I believed her. I kissed her cheeks and thanked her. Then I went to Thistle.

"You warm enough, T?"

"Yep. Thanks, Mr. Y."

"You can call me Cecil, Thistle. Seeing as how Blossom does."

"Okay . . . seems weird though."

"Yeah it kind of does. Whatever you want. You call me whatever you want then."

"Okay, Mr. Younger."

"Can I ask you something?"

"I guess."

"Have you heard anything about how Melissa Bean died, or about anybody who is going to snitch to the police?"

Suddenly Thistle's eyes filled with tears, and her breathing came fast and hard. "Aw, Mr. Younger. I don't know anything about that. Melissa was so nice and everything. I don't know anything. I really don't. I don't know anything." She cried like a little girl with big wet sobs, and her hands were shaking.

"Honey, what's wrong?" I instinctively put my hand on her forehead.

Blossom got up from her bed and wrapped her arms around her friend. "What did you say to her?" was all she said over the sobbing of her friend as I shut the bedroom door.

The next morning David called me at six and told me to meet him at the jail; Sherrie Gault had been arrested for Murder One in the death of Melissa Bean. He said he would tell me more when I got there, but there wasn't that much to tell. It was Saturday morning and the house was cold, the rain was still falling and I turned the furnace up. I put the teapot on and made a single cup of tea. Jane Marie got up, and I made her a cup of coffee. I didn't tell her about the arrest or the charges because she had to get her grant off, and if I had told her there had been an arrest in Melissa Bean's disappearance she would not have been able to concentrate. She was sitting up in bed working on her laptop and drinking her coffee when I left. I kissed her cheek and she smiled. I took my tea in a metal cup with a wide bottom and began to walk to the police station across town.

I have learned, Your Honors, that memory is not a video tape, that the impressions we store are affected by the events that come after, and yet I believe that on that morning, I had a sense that there was something broken in my life. There was something broken in the world, possibly. The rain would not stop falling, while farther to the south the forests were burning up and people's houses were exploding into bonnets of flame. Just the year before three people had been killed in a mudslide when the mountain gave way into a river of rock and trees. Fishermen were pulling up tuna on their lines offshore, and there was hardly any snow for two winters in a row. As I walked to the jail that morning, thinking about Melissa and her two small babies and about Thistle and her storm of tears the night before, I knew something was off-kilter in the world, but I didn't know what. Murder was not usually like that; murder was usually a relatively "clean" investigation because people liked to talk. I don't know if this was an actual premonition, but I like to think that on that first morning I knew everything was about to go sideways.

I shook my coat off and rubbed my fingers through my hair to shake out the rain as the dispatcher buzzed me inside. I don't think I even signed in. Cops were milling around everywhere, some in uniform, others in their civilian clothes, having come in to help out I suppose. Out in the back parking lot I saw a crime scene van open with some guys in rain gear bringing camera cases and dry bags inside. There were other cars driving away without their light bars lit.

The cops stopped talking when I came to the interview room. I knocked, said my name and walked in.

David sat at a small table across from Sherrie Gault who was in a red jumpsuit and was cuffed to the wall. I shook her left hand and sat in the corner.

"Cecil, I have been through the basics. Sherrie has been arrested on a warrant. She will likely be taken before a grand jury in a week. I doubt they will take her to a preliminary hearing. She understands not to talk with the police. She says she has not given a statement other than to ask for a lawyer and a very short denial. We will get the tapes of course. She understands our role and the protection of confidentiality that we work under. Do you have any questions about that, Sherrie? You understand that Cecil works with me, and that he is covered as well, that anything you say to him is confidential, and he cannot say or do anything that hurts your legal interests. Even if he wanted to, he cannot break his duty of confidentiality. Anything you say to him is safe. That is not true of anyone else you speak to or communicate with, you understand? They record all conversations on these jail phones. Right?"

Now, of course Your Honors, I am talking about Sherrie, but as she is currently unavailable for testimony, both in my trial and for these proceedings, an earlier court has ruled that my duty of confidentiality as per Sweeper, Sherrie as well as my co-defendants has been waived.

Back in the cell, before all the madness and killing I became involved in began, Sherrie nodded her head. Her crooked jaw was framed by her long dark hair. She was of mixed heritage: Alaskan Native, Chinese, and Pacific Islander, and she was both beautiful and fierce in appearance; a woman you both wanted to approach and from whom you would like to keep your distance.

David spoke to her about bail, which was five hundred thousand dollars total. Half of this total was to guarantee her performance, to make sure she follows the court-ordered rules. If she breaks one of the judge's rules she loses two hundred and fifty thousand dollars and goes to jail. The performance part of the bond is cash only. Cash as in, cash money: two hundred and fifty thousand dollars counted over the court clerk's desk. The appearance part of the bail can be put up by a bail bondsman for a percentage cost to the defendant. That money guarantees you show up. If you don't, the bondsman loses his dough and he sets his dogs loose on you. Sherrie hardly listened to the details and explanations of asking for a bail reduction hearing, understanding that the judge was not going to reduce her bail to anything even close to something she could come up with. Sherrie was not going to count two hundred and fifty thousand dollars over a desk. None of her family could. None of her family could ever hope to see that much cash.

We knew nothing of the facts. I could only guess

that the Sweeper had snitched on her, and Sweeper wasn't that promising of a witness, unless he could come through on the physical evidence.

There is a section of *Baby's First Felony* about the stupidity of lying to your lawyer. But to this day few clients have ever heeded this advice. *Would you lie to your doctor about your symptoms? Would you let him operate on your foot if it were really your heart that was hurting? That's what you are doing when you lie to your lawyer. You are already in a bad spot, and you only make it worse by lying to your lawyer,* was how the section read. But it didn't matter. Lying to rich people with State jobs had become a way of life for most of them.

Talking to your client for the first time, particularly in a murder investigation, is ethically . . . complex. First, there is the whole "lying thing." I think they lie because they are scared shitless, and they are still in the stage of things where they think that they can suck back the last few hours of their life, just like a little kid caught with a stolen candy bar. "No, I didn't take it." The doors may be made of steel, but they are only inches thick, and a defendant will sometimes lean against that steel door and feel the coolness of freedom on the other side. Just act like you should be let go and, who knows, maybe they will let you out. It is so tantalizing that most people just stick to an impossible lie, even with their lawyers—particularly with their lawyers, most particularly with their public defenders because they are not paying for their time.

The other complication is the lawyer doesn't want

to know too much too soon. If the client tells the lawyer a story, the client may want to stick to that story, even when the evidence completely blows it out of the water. So, we tend to wait until the evidence starts coming in to get the client's story.

But there is always the evanescent the things that will go missing. This is a pain in the ass because our clients (the guilty ones) almost always think it's okay if all the evidence goes missing, which may or may not be true. This is the thing you hate to leave to the knucklehead with the sixth-grade education, as evidenced by David's entry on page twenty-nine of *Baby's First Felony*: *Do not throw the gun purchased by your accomplice, with their fingerprints on it, into the ocean.*

To avoid knowing too much from his clients and in order to coach them on the proper theory of defense, David has me talk with them early on.

"Sherrie, I'm going to have you talk with Cecil. You remember him from before. He is going to ask you a few things. It's okay to talk with him. Okay? All right." And he walked out.

Sherrie shifted in the plastic chair. She looked at the clock where she knew the camera was located. She, too, had washed her hair, so I knew they'd had her in jail a while before they let her call. She shook her head and smiled ruefully. I let the silence settle over us like the night.

"I'm sorry, Sherrie."

"Yeah . . ." She blew out a short puff of breath.

"Are they searching your house?"

"Probably, that's okay. They won't find anything."

"Where are you living now?"

"Officially with my mom, on Biorka Street."

"But actually, where is your stuff?"

"Spread out."

"Are they searching someplace we should be worried about?"

"Not that I know of." She looked at me with sleepy eyes that I would have run from if I had any sense.

"Look, Sherrie, is there anything that is going to disappear in the next few hours that might help prove your innocence? Anything left outside that should be gathered up? Anyone leaving town who I should find right away, who could testify that you are innocent of this crime?"

She touched her finger to her lip as if she were going to turn a page, and she nodded with her chin. "Paper?"

I slid her my notebook and she wrote:

At three o'clock today go to this address, there are a couple of kids there and one of them will give you a box. Get that box. It should help. If you don't get it, I'm pretty sure it's gonna disappear.

I took a look at the address and recognized it.

"Anything else?"

"No," she said. She looked up at the clock. "Cocksuckers," she finally said, and she shook her head again, looking like a mocking angel, and yelled for the jailer to take her back to the cells.

First I went to the office to make notes and talk over

the case with David. He agreed that I should run Sherrie's errand. If there was important physical evidence in the box, I was to bring it back to the office. We had an evidence locker and some half-ass protocol that would serve as chain of custody if we ever needed to produce whatever it was in court. I downed a few cups of the bitter coffee and a stale cookie, then I went home. The girls were gone, and Jane Marie was fuming.

"Cecil, she packed her bag and left."

"Who?"

"Blossom."

"What are you talking about?"

"She says she is going to go stay with Thistle."

"You mean for the night?"

"Well, I don't know. She said all we ever do is interrogate her friends because you are some kind of narc, and she is moving in with Thistle."

"Jesus. All right, but wait, did you get your grant off?"

"Yes," she said, and she sat down at the table.

"Congratulations. That's great."

"Thank you," she said and she smiled at me, for which I was grateful. Her smile was clear and healthy, and there wasn't a drop of rain in it.

"Try not to worry about B, sweetie. Let me get something to eat, and I will call around and try to find her and bring her home. We just have to hunker down. Isn't that what one of her teachers told us? With teenagers, you just hold them close and love them no matter what, love them like it is their punishment?"

Jane Marie reached out for my hand and then she remembered: "Wait, I asked Thistle for her address when Blossom wasn't around, and she wrote it down. Let me get it." She stood up and went to her office. I walked to the kitchen and picked a cold pancake from the griddle and tore it in half. Jane Marie came back in and handed me the slip of paper with Thistle's sloppy scrawled handwriting.

"Damn it," I said as I ran toward the door.

"What?" Jane Marie called after me.

It was the same address that Sherrie had given me, but I said nothing about it to my wife, only that I would be back soon. Todd was sitting on the couch flipping through an encyclopedia, and I grabbed him to come with me. On the way out I stopped at my workbench and grabbed two pairs of leather work gloves.

We took the main road toward Old Sitka and the ferry terminal. I hadn't worn a coat, and I was soaked to the skin by the time we stood under the eaves of the second floor of the apartment complex on Halibut Point Road. What I knew about the building was that many fishery workers lived there, and a big-money card game took place at least four nights a week.

A young Filipino girl who could have been sixteen or twenty-five opened the door and stared out at us without a trace of a smile. Behind her Thistle and Blossom sat on the couch. Thistle was simply sitting, not reading or looking at anything. She appeared to be waiting for something, but she had a very worried expression on her face that did not improve at all when she recognized Todd and me. Blossom was staring at her laptop and phone simultaneously.

"Hello . . . um . . . Mr. Younger." Thistle got up quickly from the couch and put her hand on the back of the girl/woman at the door. "Are you here about Sherrie?"

"Yes. I am."

"She called me and told me someone from her lawyer's office would be coming by for something. She told me to give it to you. Hold on." And she disappeared.

I turned to my daughter. "Blossom, come on, get your stuff we've got to go."

"I'm doing homework, if you must know." It was only then I recognized the music blaring in the background: the Mountain Goats. "I'm not coming home. I have to do a PowerPoint presentation for science class, I'm doing it on Chavo Guerrero, the Mexican wrestler."

"Wait a minute, what? For *science* class?"

Thistle returned carrying a cardboard box, one of the largest prepaid priority mailers. It was encased in clear tape as if someone wanted it to be waterproof. Thistle handed it to me. "She said you were not to open it here," she said in her thin, worried voice.

"What's in it?"

"I have no idea. It was way back under my bed behind a bunch of other stuff. Some other guy already came around looking for it today, but we didn't let him in."

"Who, Emily?"

She told me the Sweeper's real name.

"So he knows about this box?"

"I don't know for sure. He just asked for the thing that Sherrie kept for the lawyer, and he said he wanted it. I didn't let him in. He's creepy. I never liked him. He's mean. He was always mean to Sherrie. 'Specially after she called the cops on him for hitting her all those times."

"All right, Thistle—Emily . . . You should go back to your mom. If you can't do that you can stay with us." I stopped speaking and looked at Thistle who was thinner now than I remembered her being last school year, and she scratched her arm nervously. She was becoming a ghost, Your Honors, or so I believed then.

"Girls, does Sherrie Gault live here? Did she live here when she was out of jail?"

"No, not really, Mr. Younger. She just keeps some stuff here. Sometimes when the card games go late she sleeps here, that's all."

"We are fine right here, Cecil," Blossom said loudly, not taking her eyes off her computer. "And yes, it's a science class, the unit this semester is on edges and boundaries. So I chose the US–Mexican border. I got the teacher's permission and everything."

"No, Blossom. You are coming home. It's not up for discussion. Come on. Close up the computer. Todd, put your gloves on. Thistle, did she have a bag?"

Thistle looked around and nodded to a waterproof

duffel, I threw some books and some cords that were scattered around into the bag and zipped it. I had the mailer under my arm and carried the bag in the same hand.

"Come on, girly . . . Let's go. Todd, give her a hand." And we took her by the elbows out of the apartment. At first she tried to bite me. Then she whined. She threatened to break her computer, but I called her bluff, telling her it was fine with me if she broke it, but I was not buying another. We stopped and put the computer in the bag, and she made me carry it as her final act of resistance. She cursed me and pulled against me but did nothing to resist Todd.

She broke free from our grip once we got home, grabbed her bag, ran to her room and slammed the door. Todd, who was oblivious of the emotional charge of the incident, went back to reading his encyclopedia, which I noticed was the letter *S* of the old Britannica set I had inherited from my father as a boy. I took the box upstairs. Jane Marie was at the table working at her computer. She seemed pleased to know our daughter was home from the gambling den and the hang out of an accused child abductor and murderer, but to be fair she didn't know all those facts.

"David called. He said Sherrie Gault was arraigned and got assigned to you guys on a murder charge. He wants you to call him." Her eyes scanned an email.

I took out my pocketknife and started cutting through the layers of tape around the box. The thumping of the Screaming Females leaked through the floorboards of our little house, and the clattering of books hitting wood punctuated the song.

I tore off the lid of the box and saw the money: stacks of hundreds and fifties joined with rubber bands. It looked like each band had about twenty-five hundred bucks, and there were twenty of them. The bills were worn. Some looked as if they had been curled. Some were stiff and fresh but not numbered or sequential. On top of the bundle of cash was a note reading:

> *If you are reading this you know what to do.*
> *That motherfucker has to be taken care of.*

I took the box to Jane Marie's office and rummaged her drawers for some packing tape. I resealed the box with the note inside. I put the box in a black garbage bag and then into an old suitcase of my father's that was on the bookshelf. I told Jane Marie I had to run to the grocery store and took the money down the street to the break room in the cold storage, where there is a phone the workers can use to make local calls. Hundreds of people use the phone: those who don't use their cell phones, anyway. I picked up the receiver, called David and told him to come to the cold storage, so I could show him what it was I had in my possession. I did not want to speak for long on the phone. I waited across the street in the rain, watching the workers from the plant come out for their break and into the covered outdoor smoking area. Men and women in rain gear and rubber boots, many with bandannas wrapped around their hair, they leaned against the plywood walls and swapped their lighters. Some poured coffee from stainless steel containers. Every time someone glanced my way, I tried not to think about what was in the case at my feet. I felt suddenly awkward carrying the suitcase, as if it were beginning to glow.

Finally, David drove up in his shiny Subaru station wagon. I hopped in the front passenger seat and put the case on my lap. I showed him the box and described what was in it.

"Holy shit," he said, finally.

We sat motionless in the car for a few moments. Then he became aware of the workers watching us, parked where we shouldn't be, right where the forklifts drove boxes of frozen fish around the plant. He pulled out onto the narrow waterfront street.

"Let me think," he said as he drove.

Ravens and gulls sat on the rooflines of the corrugated tin roofs. Men with bloody aprons pushed hand trucks across the streets.

"Take it back," he said.

"I'm not taking it back," I told him. "Sweeper has been snooping around for it. It's just teenage kids living in that apartment."

"That is not your problem. Having this cash is your problem. You can't keep it. Our client just swore to the judge that she was indigent, for one thing. The second thing, the note, may be construed as a threat against a witness."

"Arguably . . . yes . . . It doesn't require too much imagination."

"Cecil. You have to take it back. I don't even want you to know anything about this box. I don't want to look at the box. For God's sake, don't open it again. Don't talk about it. Just take it back, give it to the girls and forget you ever saw it."

A half hour later, Your Honors, I have to say that the box with the fifty thousand dollars and the note wanting me to "take care of" some motherfucker was still in the black garbage bag and suitcase and sitting in between some extra bags of insulation in the ceiling of my house. I was sitting with Sherrie Gault in the jail.

"Don't you have a car?" She looked at my wet hair and the front of my shirt, which was sticking to my skin.

"I don't drive."

"Don't you get tired of being wet?"

"I get tired of walking around in the rain with a box full of fifty thousand dollars."

"Huh?" she deadpanned.

"Sherrie, what the hell?" I took out a pencil and my Rite in the Rain notebook from my pocket, knowing she didn't trust the microphones in the interview room.

WHAT IS THE MONEY FOR? I wrote, then slid it over where she could see it.

She considered my notebook for perhaps thirty seconds, then took the pencil. *IT IS FOR COVERING THE PROBLEM OF* [here she used Sweeper's real name] *'S TESTIMONY.* She slid the notebook back toward me.

I wrote: *COVER? WHAT DO YOU MEAN COVER?*

She was much faster this time: *YOU ARE THE EXPERT IN THESE THINGS. YOU KNOW.*

I was much quicker too: *I AM NOT GOING TO COMMIT A CRIME UNDER ANY CIRCUMSTANCES, SO GET THAT OUT OF YOUR HEAD.*

She almost grabbed the pencil out of my hand. *NO, NO . . . THAT'S NOT WHAT I MEANT AT ALL! I JUST MEANT TO HELP WITH MY CASE, HIRE EXPERTS OR NEEDED EXPENSES IF THE PUBLIC DEFENDER WON'T COME UP WITH EXPENSES.* She looked at me, and her eyes were soft and slightly wet with tears as if she were actually remorseful and saddened by my misunderstanding. Her mouth was set hard, her jaw clenched.

No matter what she had written, there was no doubt in my mind that she wanted me, or someone, to kill Sweeper.

"What's the chance of him recanting?" I asked her.

"I don't know." She shook her head. Now her voice was hard. No pretense. "Slim to none."

"What if that was where we put our resources, instead of with experts, know what I'm saying?"

She nodded and leaned forward. With her free hand, she motioned to me to lean in to block the camera view.

"He wants in to the game. He's got ambition, and besides, now he's scared. Money's not enough."

"Not enough money, you mean?"

"Naw . . . he's scared and greedy. Only one thing cures that."

"What's that?"

Here, Your Honors she made an enigmatic gesture: she pantomimed a gun with her finger and pointed it at her head and pulled the trigger, then she pointed it at the clock where the police had hidden a camera.

"But I'm counting on you to take care of this, Cecil. You my boy." She reached out and touched my knee.

Just as I was about to give her my speech again about how I was not going to commit any crimes while investigating her case, there was a knock on the interview room door and Hank the jailer came barreling in.

"Got to get meals, Cecil. Time to wrap it up. Besides the LT wants to talk with you."

I left Sherrie chained to the wall. In the hall by the locked door that led outside, the lieutenant put his hand on my chest to stop me, though he didn't need to. His tie was pulled down, his shirt unbuttoned, and he had a two-day growth of beard. His thick glasses looked smudged and dirty.

"Cecil, we want to ship her out of here soon, get her over to Juneau. Do you guys think she is going to be asking for a hearing in the next few days?"

"I can't tell you, Lieutenant, but I agree. I think it would be good for her to be in Juneau. I will have you talk with David as soon as possible. Why do you want her out of here? Is she a problem?"

He took his glasses off and wiped his eyes, and I could see the red rims under his lids. "Naw, just some loose chatter around some of her associates . . . bunch of rascals. You know how it is." He put his glasses back on, then swung the heavy door open for me and labored to keep it open until I walked out.

The rain had stopped momentarily, and the wind carried the faint smell of the sea. Straight overhead, the sky was blue, and I could hear gulls calling above the harbor. A fat raven with a black cookie in its beak stood on the lip of a municipal garbage bin that was propped open. It bobbed on its twig legs and twisted its head one way and then another suspiciously, as if it was certain I was going to snatch the cookie away. As I approached, it bobbed deep, and the lionlike mane flared before the bird bobbed again, then lifted into the air and flew away with its plunder. Just as the raven crested out over the harbor, the clouds covered the sun and rain began falling again.

David was sitting with his feet up, and his eyes were closed tight when I walked in. "Cecil, if our clients weren't complicated and messed up in the first place, we probably would never have met them."

He paused, and the rain spat at his window. "This fucking weather," he muttered. David had grown up in Virginia, near Washington, DC, and he took the constant rain as a personal taunt.

"You can't keep the money," he continued. "That

is obvious. You have two choices. You either have to take the money back to the place you got it. Record yourself doing it. Leave a receipt and have whoever is there sign the receipt. If they don't, just make sure you record that you left it along with a receipt . . .

"Or . . . Or . . . You can put it in a paper bag, walk up to the police station and say 'pursuant to evidence rule six point two, I'm giving you this bag.' Then you walk out.

"But I don't recommend that because it will probably mess up our client, whose fingerprints are probably all over those bills, and no . . . we cannot clean the bills because that would be tampering with evidence."

There is a section of *Baby's First Felony* that covers incriminating physical evidence and discusses hiding places in relatively public areas or shared living spaces because their very existence cannot be traced to you. Believe it or not, a good old hole in the ground somewhere there are no cameras or digging animals is still the best bank for illegal cash, if you don't have a crooked lawyer with a safe. One of the more ingenious meth labs was built out on a fishing boat that had a tilt table that could dump the entire process into the bay at the first sign of trouble, but most of our clients can't afford a boat, and if they can, they try to fish them, which in some years was better than making meth. Safer at least.

"If I do nothing?" I was standing next to the window, watching the intersecting rings in the pond-size puddles in the parking lot.

"If you do nothing, you arguably are part of a criminal conspiracy to suborn perjury . . . with her in the jail . . . They say they can't, but you and I know they can probably 'miraculously find' the audio of your jail visit."

"What I really want to know is when did the girl get so gangster? Killing the Sweeper? Really? And where did she get so much cash up front? This is Sitka, for God's sake, this is the home of drunken domestic battlebots, not Scarface."

David opened his eyes and smiled. "Our little girl is all grown up." He glanced out the window again and frowned, then he gestured to the more than fifty open files in dividers on his desk. "People are saying there is new meth in town. The junkies are saying someone new has started a lab. They say the new stuff is good. But our kids don't have the money to start a lab. Or didn't . . . The meth had been coming from Mexico in dribs and drabs, and from the small-scale tweaker labs until they cracked down on all the ingredients: phosphorus scratch pads and pseudoephedrine. The old stuff smelled like gas and gave you headaches. This new stuff is apparently clean and gives you an appetite for sweets."

"Nice to know, Dave."

"Just saying . . . and the first five hits are free."

"Shut the front door . . ."

"Truth . . . Well, street truth, you know what I'm saying? They are all saying it: the first five hits are free."

"That's smart money right there. That's some

serious, cynical investment money talking. Not junkie
money."

"I'm afraid so."

I started walking to my office when my named co-
defendant, Mr. Robert Boomer, came in. Mr. Boomer
was notorious for not making or keeping his appoint-
ments and dropping in unannounced. Mr. Boomer
currently had felony DUI charges, and his history
included multiple assaults and explosives and weapons
charges. It is believed that as a child, he was inspired
by his last name to begin blowing things up. He soon
discovered that he enjoyed it. There is a chapter in
Baby's First Felony dedicated to Robert Boomer entitled,
"When Confessing to an Explosives Charge, Try Not to
Say 'Awesome' in Every Sentence."

"Cecil," Robert said, bowing at the waist with some
difficulty because of his girth.

"Robert," I answered, "I have very little time, but
what do you need?" This was how all of these drop-ins
started. Mr. Boomer would eat up hours until David
would throw him out. I didn't have the heart, and Mr.
Boomer always had interesting tidbits of lore from
the CM, or "Criminal Milieu," as he would refer to
his circle of associates. Some of his information was
hallucinatory, conspiracy-minded rage aimed at the
authorities. Other accounts might actually describe
events he had witnessed, and some might have been
willful lies he fed me, believing as he did that the Public
Defender Agency was the ass-end of the great, corrupt
sausage-making machine that was the criminal justice

system, and by giving us false information he was in a sense throwing a wooden shoe into the machinery.

"Cecil . . . I would like you to find the Stanford behavioral study which proved that any person given authority over others in a jail-like situation will eventually abuse their power and became physically cruel."

"All right, Robert, and we want this in your DUI case?"

"Fuck, yes!" He looked over at Rhonda who was date-stamping some incoming mail. "Excuse my French, Rhonda."

Rhonda, who despite being a devout Catholic has heard more rough talk than most loggers or rodeo cowboys, waved her hand and said, "That's a quarter," and pointed to the inappropriately labeled FUCK IT BUCKET, where we put our cursing quarters. Robert dug into his grease-encrusted coveralls, found a quarter, then flipped it in.

"I have heard of this Stanford study, Robert. Grad students pretended to be guards and prisoners and the student guards started to abuse the student prisoners."

"Exactly."

"You want us to bring the professor from Stanford to testify as to whether you were under the influence when you were operating your vehicle?"

"No. I want to show the jury that the cops are cruel and vicious assholes, and they have a scientific reason to be."

"I'll talk with David." This was the only way to answer Robert Boomer. To say no and tell him he was crazy was to invite a much, much longer discussion.

"You are the best, Cecil." Robert smiled at me.

Rhonda was pointing back and forth toward the door and David's office. Indicating Robert was closing in on his no-appointment time limit. Also, Rhonda could not bear Robert Boomer's personal hygiene, which was spectacularly eccentric for a person with a home. He worked on heavy equipment and never, ever washed his work clothes since "they will just get dirty again." His coveralls were spectacularly grimy, and his wool long underwear, which had started off white, was an oily charcoal grey. Robert also ran metal lathe band saws, so his coveralls were caked with iron filings and chips of various industrial material. He smelled of unknown liquid waste. He was bald and his head was streaked with various substances. For comfort Robert wore a silk woman's nightshirt under his long underwear, and often he would douse himself with some old cologne that blended with the Vaseline and chili pepper mixture that he combined with dimethyl sulfoxide to help absorption, and lathered on his legs for muscle pain. If any of Your Honors have been to the chemical plants in the wetlands outside of Secaucus, New Jersey, this is the closest thing that I can think of that Robert Boomer smelled like. Rhonda wanted him out, but I wanted to talk with him.

I got him in my office and closed the door. "What have you heard about the new meth in town?"

"You want to buy a clean gun, Cecil?"

"What are you talking about?"

"I hear there is going to be a war coming. The Mexicans are pissed off."

"Who is behind all this meth?"

"Your girl, Sherrie. That's the word."

"She doesn't have that kind of money."

"She does now. I'm buying up ammo, man. I'm not shitting you. I'm stocking up all kinds of shit."

"You have to stay out of trouble until your trial. You know that, Robert. We have good motions on your stop, we have a chance to get you out of felony land."

Robert was a frequent flyer with the Public Defender Agency; he knew exactly what I was talking about when I said "motions on your stop." The best way to beat a drunk driving case is to file a motion saying that the original stop of the vehicle by the police was unwarranted or illegal. To drunk drivers, the law on illegal stops is like the Magna Carta, right behind the sacred second amendment right to carry weapons at all times.

"I'm not giving up my fucking right to self-defense, you crazy?"

"So, who is behind Sherrie?"

"The city . . . the cops, man, that new lieutenant is a corrupt bastard, I'm telling you."

"Stop it."

"I know. No one wants to believe it. That's why it makes perfect sense."

"You need something more than unbelievability on your side." I tapped on my desk and stood up.

"Cecil . . . If we could prove that the cops were deeply corrupt and into the drug business, would that help my case?"

I thought about it long and hard. Robert Boomer was not stupid. You never want to lie to someone like him, or he will be all over you for the rest of your life. "Is there a tie in with you and this drug business?"

"Only in that I've been trying to get the troopers and the ombudsman to investigate the corruption in the local police force for-fucking-ever and they have refused."

"Do you think they trumped up these charges because of their dealings in drugs, sex and gambling?"

"It's possible," he said looking at me steadily.

This was the right answer on his part; he was not overselling his position.

"Then it is possible that evidence of corruption could help us attack the affidavits and warrants that were served in your case. It might even help us if we could get it in at trial, but that is much less clear and you would have to talk with David about that. It would depend on the information, how solid it is and how it ties to your case. I'm sorry, all I can tell you is a solid 'maybe.'"

He smiled at me and clapped his hands together, then said, "Then I can tell you that 'maybe' there will be a Mexican man coming to Sitka at the end of the week, and he will be trying to consolidate his business holdings here, and he is going to be asking the exact same questions that you are."

"Where the new meth is coming from?"

"Exactly," Robert said as he picked a quarter-inch iron filing from the greasy fluff of his undershirt.

"Would he talk with me?"

"I haven't gone to law school, but I'm confident that I can still give you a solid, 'maybe.'" Then Robert Boomer gave me a hug, the aftermath of which lingered on my clothes for days afterward.

Two days and several dozen phone calls later, Your Honors, Mr. Boomer and I were waiting outside of the Sitka airport for "the Mexican." Through information from various clients, NOT Mr. Boomer, I found out that a supplier from Yakima, Washington, was coming to town, and he knew that I was friends with a good friend of his who had moved back to Mexico. I had helped this mutual friend with some serious charges and the courier had agreed to meet me. I agreed not to ask him any questions about his business, but he would give me any information that he knew about his competitors' business in exchange for complete anonymity. I understood that he was not staying the night in our town. I was not to know his name. I was not to ask for any personal information. I was not to take photographs or have a phone or camera with me when I spoke with him. I was simply looking for information about our current client and seeing if the Mexican knew anything about the new drug traffickers in our little town. This was my only intention, Your Honors, to do my job as an investigator.

When he stepped outside he raised his collar to the

rain and scowled as if someone were spitting on him. He was a thin man with dark hair. He had a small mesh grocery bag over his shoulder that looked like it held a bottle of soda and some beef jerky. He had nothing else. He wore nice western-style boots and a snap-button shirt under his expensive leather jacket. He looked both left and right, paused when looking to his right and walked immediately to a waiting cab. I looked to my left and saw an undercover detective sitting in an unmarked Ford Explorer. As the cab pulled out, so too did the Explorer. Our little convoy drove to the waterfront where the Mexican checked in to the only waterfront hotel by a harbor. Mr. Boomer dropped me around the corner and went home, and I doubled back with a slim biography of Herman Melville that I had started reading and a coparenting manual that Jane Marie had given me called, *The Challenging Teen* by Dr. Anne Talbot. I took both books and went back to the coffee bar off the hotel lobby, which gave a good view of the stairwell and the elevator, then made camp.

Your Honors, this may seem like a gross digression, but trust me; it has a bearing on my pleading. What I love about Melville is not that he was a genius, but that some mysterious force in Nature moved him. Melville knew how to yearn. Melville knew how to live with beauty and without answers. When, as a young man, he set sail on a whaler for a year and a half and then jumped ship, he was changed by what he saw; the sea, the animals and the vastness of the mystery left him altered and without firm judgment of others. This is why you can read and reread *Moby Dick*. He let it be mystery.

But out of respect for my wife, I picked up Dr. Talbot and started reading:

> *Kids today are faced with overwhelming choices, and their acting out is a siren song for help. We can often help them most, not by giving them something more, which is our first instinct, but by limiting, with focusing their choices to a healthy few.*

I closed the book and looked at the cover. I wondered if there was enough time to go back to the bookstore and get our money back.

In two hours, the Mexican came down out of the elevator. He looked at me, then looked at something on his phone, then at me again. "You for me?"

"Yes, sir." I stood up.

"Come." We walked down the hall inside the hotel to a clothing store where he bought rain gear and cheap rubber boots. He left his good boots and jacket in a plastic bag at the desk of the hotel. He pantomimed that he would pick it up soon, by pointing at his wrist. The clerk was amiable and tucked the bag away.

Out of his pocket he took an old trucker's cap and a bandanna. He wrapped his bandanna around his head and then put the old billed cap on backward. Now he looked like any number of new employees of the fish plant that rumbled night and day just down the street from my house and the hotel.

He walked to the time clock and grabbed a badge. I couldn't tell if he carefully selected one, or if he grabbed a Hispanic name at random. He pinned it on and walked into the plant. I grabbed a visitors badge and a hairnet. I had been to the plant hundreds of times over the years to talk to people and knew the drill. Inside is a dripping, echoing sea food factory: cold water and fish smell, bloody slush ice on the floor, batteries overcharging and forklift backup alarms sounding. My man went to another man and they went to a corner to talk. The one gave my man a slip of paper and a key. He also gave him a large knife and a small hatchet. We went to a locker reserved for various fishing boats inside the freezer. The air was sticky in the subzero temperature. Inside the freezer locker were twenty boxes of frozen salmon that my man sorted through. He pointed and gestured for me to pull out some fish. He knelt on the floor. The fish I pulled out had some twine along their bellies. My man was strong and good with tools. He pried the frozen flesh away and cut the two knots in the twine: one by the head and one closer to the anal fin. Then he took the hatchet and with three blows he chopped the head off, stood up and swung the tail hard toward the floor and a stiff, white packet wrapped in canvas popped out.

Ten fish, ten packets, each about two pounds in weight. They looked like wrapped meat. He put the mangled fish in a separate box. The packets went in his net bag, and we walked away.

The police and TSA had caught their fair share of drug mules coming into the country by plane. The post office had sniffing dogs. No one had thought to concentrate on the fishing fleet. It was clear that someone was bringing drugs up the coast and handing them to fishermen offshore. The fishermen would unload all their fish to the cold storages, and with the help of selected workers the fish with drugs stuffed into their bellies would be frozen and stored. No sniffing dogs. No camera surveillance, and no drama to draw attention from the police. Later I learned that the cartel used a crab boat from the Bering Sea Fishery for their workboat, and it stuck out in Southeastern, but they fixed it later.

The Mexican walked ahead of me, back to the hotel. He took off his bandanna and threw it in the trash. He took off his raincoat as he turned the corner and now he could easily pass for a prosperous European charter fisherman. He walked past a white man sweeping the covered sidewalk in front of the hotel.

That man was Wynn Sanders, the owner of the hotel who had lost his daughter to drugs and offered to post bail for some of our clients, including the Sweeper. I watched my man walk past Mr. Sanders, then into the hotel. I waited perhaps two minutes by walking to the city hall across the square next to the sea wall, and then back again. I walked up to Mr. Sanders.

"Mister Younger," he said in a courtly way, not taking his attention away from his sweeping.

"Mr. Sanders, how are you, sir?" I said and I smiled at him.

"I'm staying out of trouble, sir. You?" He kept his eyes on the garbage that his broom gathered: dirt and gum wrappers, bottle caps and spruce needles coated with mud. "You appear to me to be the type of man that may be courting disaster, Mr. Younger," and here he lifted his Stetson hat and adjusted it, slightly exposing his thinning hair. He squinted through his glasses as he stared at me.

"I spoke with Sweeper and Ms. Gault. I imagine you have heard of their problems?"

"No, sir." he said. "I haven't and I don't plan to."

"All right, sir. I understand that. It's just David told me that you had offered to put up bail."

"There is no need to be obsequious, Mr. Younger. At one time it was possible for me to help the girl, but now there is no need. Things change. That's all."

"I understand," I said and I did. Bailing out junkies is a bad investment with a low return.

"I find drug addicts wearing on my nerves. Don't you?" he asked. Then looked back inside to where his bellman appeared to be lazily talking on his cell phone with one elbow on the check-in counter. "Excuse me, Mr. Younger. You take good care of yourself now," he said, as if he had not said anything at all. But then he turned back, "And please, be careful, will you?" Then he walked inside.

The bellman was getting chewed out as I walked by. The elevator was stopped on the fourth floor; I could tell from the lobby indicator. I walked up the stairs to the fourth floor and walked down the hall looking for my man. I came to an open door in the middle of the hall. He had taken off his rain gear and put on his traveling clothes. He grabbed another key card from under the telephone. We left the rain gear in the first room and went down the stairs to another, larger corner room. In that room, there was whiskey, tequila and a full ice bucket. There was also a nine-millimeter handgun under one of the chair cushions. My man looked at his Timex watch, opened the window, set the bag on the windowsill, jacked a round into the chamber, sat in the chair and looked at me as if he had been waiting all day for me to start talking.

"So?" he said.

"Can we talk now?"

He spoke with a thick accent, but it was clear he had no problem understanding. He was perhaps in his forties, now that I got a good look at him with the light on his face. He had a tough countenance, and his eyes were brown but vacant as he stared directly at me.

"We have some time, but there will be people coming soon. You will have to go before that." He stood up and looked out the window. He nodded to someone who was apparently in the parking lot on the harbor side, three stories below. "The police may come to the room upstairs. Not here. If they come here, zip . . ."

and he made a gesture of throwing something out the window. "They find nothing."

"The drugs go in the harbor?"

"To be fished out . . . There are fishermen here, yes?" He smiles, then sits down again and arranges the nine-millimeter as if it were a drink on a coaster. "People will come." He looked at his watch.

"Do you know who your new competitors are in our little town?"

He grimaced, "*Mierda.* This town is shit. I don't care. This place is dinky . . . Yes?"

"Yes. Dinky."

"But some *pendejo* is talking disrespectfully, foolishly. All gangster. Ridiculous." He said "gangster" as if he were parodying someone on television I didn't recognize. "Someone is talking violence to my customers. Making threats. Stupid. This is America. We have a product and a price, let them beat it. Let them give better service and what?"

"Quality?"

"*Exactamente.* But these people make threats to my customers. Tell them not to buy from me anymore. Ridiculous. I don't need to come here. Is this a joke? How can it be? Sir, I cannot allow my employees to be threatened and scared off. *No es possible.*"

There was a light knock on the door. My man looked at his wristwatch and scowled. He put his finger to his lips.

The knock came again. No voice. Then a slide in the door lock.

The Mexican was up in an instant, and the net bags and the drugs were out the window. I backed up toward the bathroom and my man went to the door, which was opening slowly. The Mexican raised his handgun and before it came past his waist, a blast filled the room, and crimson brain matter spattered all the way back to the window.

The Mexican fell hard on the carpet. His skull was misshapen and looked like a melted rubber mask of his face. The room smelled of cordite and fresh blood. No one came through the door. I ran to the window and saw bubbles blossoming on the dark water of the boat harbor. There was a diver in the water. In the parking lot there was a rental car with blood spattered on the inside of the windshield, and a hand dangled out of the driver's side window. No one else moved.

I wiped down everything I had touched with a towel from the bathroom, and I left the room. As I turned to take one last look, the gauzy curtain was billowing out of the open window, and the Mexican lay as still as an anvil tipped over on the carpet. Then I walked slowly down the hall to the stairwell. There were no security cameras that I noticed, but I didn't stop to chat at the desk. I walked straight home down Katlian Street. This is the truth, Your Honors. I had nothing to do with the shootings at the hotel.

When I arrived home, Todd was on the street in front of our house, and my gut went into a spasm. Todd saw me and waved, then walked quickly toward me.

"Todd, what's wrong?"

He stopped some two feet from me, breathing hard. "Cecil, some men told me a joke at the Pioneer today and I told it and I think that some people are very upset."

"Is that it, Todd? A joke?"

"Well, Cecil, you see they are pretty mad."

I gave him a hug, which I rarely ever do, and I think this confused him. "Good," I said which must have confused him more. As we turned to go toward the house, I said, "I don't have time to hear it now. I have things to do."

"What's green and melts in your mouth?" Todd blurted out, ignoring me.

"I don't know."

"A leper's dick."

"Oh, for fuck's sake, Todd!"

He slumped his shoulders as we walked through the door. "I don't understand it at all, Cecil."

"It's a terrible joke, buddy . . . on so many levels . . . I don't really want to talk about it. Just never tell it again."

"Never tell what again?" Jane Marie asked from the top of the stairs.

Now, Your Honors, I know you might be wondering why in the world I would mention any of this, but you see, context is everything, and for you to understand what came before and after, you should know the speed at which things were changing and how confusing the rest of my life had become.

Jane Marie was upstairs with her friend Liz. There

was no way I could talk about the shooting I had witnessed. No one could know. I was hoping they were in deep conversation so I could slip past them and into our room for a shower and a change of clothes.

"Cecil." Jane Marie stopped me in my tracks. "What's that on your pants?" I looked down and big as life, I swear to God, was a square inch of liver-colored brain matter from the Mexican's skull, caught in a smear of blood.

"Oh, shit," I said grabbing a paper towel as quickly as I possibly could and wiping it off. "I . . . I was going by the harbor, and Clyde was loading a deer up the dock. He had been hunting in his skiff, and I helped him throw the carcass in his truck. It's nothing."

She looked at me nonplussed and stayed quiet until I realized that the only thing that was suspicious was I was acting a little too fastidious about my pants. So, I dropped the chunk and the bloody towel in the garbage can and gave her a kiss.

"Where's B?" I asked her.

"I don't know. I haven't heard from her. She was supposed to be coming home from Thistle's. Liz and I were just talking about getting this next grant and maybe hiring Blossom to work in the field with us this summer. You think she would like that?"

"Not right now . . . but maybe by summer." I gestured toward the bedroom. "I'll go over there and get her as soon as I take a shower. That buck must have been in rut or something." I pantomimed a terrible smell reaction.

Liz put her tea mug down and held her nose and then sat up straight. "Cecil, you really need to keep Blossom out of that apartment house."

"Why's that, Liz?"

"Ernie was doing some work over there. The roof leaks for one thing, and the place is a wreck. But he says there are some shady goings on, and Ernie knows shady."

Ernie had done time in a military brig in the seventies and lived under the docks in Ketchikan in the eighties. Liz was right. He knew shady.

"What did he say?"

"I was just telling Jane Marie: card games where . . . He says the house provides the big winners young girls to keep them playing. Ernie says that he has heard about this but hasn't seen it himself."

"Are you saying the girls are turning tricks?"

"Ernie wouldn't tell me."

"Cecil!" Jane Marie piped up with the one word that was clearly an urgent request. "Go get her. Please."

I quickly showered. My hair was still wet, I took our household garbage and stuffed it in a backpack along with my clothes from the morning. I walked about a mile and a half to the transfer station, said hello to Pig-nose Bob who works there and asked if any new treasures had come through. I tossed my household junk with the Mexican's brain matter on my pants into the van to be loaded onto the barge and shipped off the island to the deserts of eastern Washington. We talked about the Gibson jazz guitar he pulled out of the trash and the next gig his band was going to play. Just before I left I mentioned the time and told him it was an hour earlier than it actually was. He didn't wear a watch. He would remember me coming by and hopefully give me an hour of dead time to an alibi that I might need.

Even as water plastered our hair against our skulls, we did not mention the rain.

After leaving the transfer station I walked to the Public Defender Agency office. Rhonda was talking on the phone and two other lines were ringing. My other co-defendant, Gudger Whelks, sat in my office chair. Rhonda pointed at him while she cradled the receiver against her ear and pantomimed that he had been waiting for me, and there was nothing she could do.

Gudger was in his thirties but he looked much older. Alcoholism had aged him prematurely. He was thin and gaunt now. As a child he had been bright-eyed and mischievous. He had been funny, and a fine fisherman; he had a good arm and could throw anything straight and true: rocks, dirt clods, or snow-balls. No deserted house could save its windows from Gudger's arm. He had pitched for our state high school baseball team and had his picture on the Wall of Champions at the school district office, but he was now known in the system as an "unsheltered inebriate," that is, he slept in the woods or on derelict boats, or surfed the floors and couches in the drunk houses that popped up around town. Gudger's family had given up on him. Their tough love had found its limit, and now they waited like mourners for him to either die or hit his psychic "bottom," but Gudger was Herculean in his ability to suffer. Lesser men would have found bottom years before, with the arrests and suicide attempts, the beatings and the mornings waking up, bloody and soaked in his own urine, on a hard piece of concrete. Some said his brain was damaged so that no matter how badly he hurt himself from alcohol, his first instinct when he found himself alive was to start looking for a drink. But no matter how hard he fell, I could still recognize the young man in him, and truthfully, Your Honors, I never gave up hope that he would someday be able to experience another sober day, and then two, then perhaps a lifetime.

He was facing a light charge of trespassing. He had been banned from almost every commercial establishment in Sitka and not a few of the churches. David had argued in court that it would take a sober and expert cartographer to navigate town with all the restrictions laid out for Gudger. Of course, it wasn't the charges that were the problem; it was the probation violation that would bring him the jail time. The state of Alaska had come to an impasse with Gudger, they didn't want him in jail; they wanted him sober, and the only hammer they had to hold over his head to get him into treatment was more and more jail time. Now for a man of his superhuman tolerance for pain and adverse living situations, even two months of jail time wasn't that much of a deterrent. There would be the pain of detox and the sickness, the weakness, nausea, dehydration, cramps and seizures, but really, that's what jail was for, a pit stop for the serious drinking man. Young ballers did cocaine to keep from drinking. Gudger did short stints in jail.

I had bought him meals and found him jobs and vouched for his character. Once or twice I had even bribed him to get alcohol treatment. He had done the thirty-day treatment seven times. He had been recommended for a long-term program but could not afford it. He was of mixed heritage from some Pacific Island nation, Tlingit and a mean Norwegian fisherman. His sister and his mother would only feed him if he came to church with them. His father had walked off a dock and drowned after a night of drinking that lasted six weeks.

Gudger looked up at me. "What are we doing on my case?"

"The offer has not changed: long-term treatment or three months in jail."

He sniffed. He was drunk. I shook his hand. His grip was warm-water soft and he had the perfumy stink of acetone and composted flowers.

"You working?" I looked at him, and he had added to the collection of scars on his face, fresh scabs that could have been made with a knife. I didn't ask about those.

"I got some work over at the old Hillside Apartments. They are fixing the roof."

"You think you could save some money in the next

few months? Just enough for food and travel, enough to get into treatment, if we found you a bed?"

"Man . . . Cecil . . ." He looked at his wet leather shoes and squeezed some rainwater from the sleeve of his sloppy, wet leather coat. The water pooled brown on the carpet. "Let's not argue."

I actually appreciated this. The one thing that gave me hope about Gudger was that deep down, he knew himself and he knew me. He knew that we weren't going to go around and around trying to fool each other.

"You really got a job over there?"

"Yes."

"Then what are you doing here?"

"I didn't say I had started."

"Well, my daughter is supposed to be there now, and I've got to go. I might need a hand. Let's go." I walked back into David's office and took the suitcase that held the fifty thousand dollars. I had moved it to our locked evidence cabinet earlier that day. David tipped back in his chair, away from his computer, and looked at me.

"Is that going home?"

"Yes," I said.

"Good" was all he said as he turned back to the motion he was writing.

I grabbed a tape recorder and a camera and walked out the door with my drunken client and the fifty grand.

Your Honors, David was right, the money had to go

back. Nothing good was going to happen for Sherrie Gault with this money. Nothing good would come of it for her or for me. The only thing that money could buy was new charges in terms of her legal case. But right then I was thinking of several things, and only one of them was Sherrie Gault's legal defense. On that day, at that moment, Your Honors, I was thinking of who I could motivate with this money. I was thinking of protecting Thistle and Blossom. If the money went back, the girls had to come out. I knew even then they were sleeping in the ante room of a slaughter house.

As we walked by the waterfront hotel, there were no blue lights, no ambulance, and no sign of alarm. The car that appeared to have the blood spatter on the windshield and the corpse-like hand out the window was gone. The window to the room where the Mexican had been shot was closed and the shades drawn. I said nothing to Gudger about any of it. He noticed nothing about what was going through my mind, or the nervous expression on my face, but walked with his feet wide apart and his determined drunkard's stare like headlights, straight ahead.

Standing across the street from the Hillside Apartments, where the legendary card games were held and I assumed my only daughter was staring into her phone, the building appeared to have a southeastern cant. It had been framed by twelve by twelve fir timbers that had allegedly been brought up to Alaska at the turn of the last century to serve as support timbers for several of the gold mines in the area. Juneau was producing gold after the Klondike had played out. The mines in Sitka found color and then investors, and the timber came up on ships from the woods of northern Washington, but the investors were being swindled. The mines had been salted with gold by their original claimants, who sold the claims, then took off for parts unknown, leaving the timber on the docks with the new investors and no profitable holes to dig. So, the timbers were first turned into a hotel, then the building became a laundromat and a store, and then the old heap became a sagging apartment house for itinerant workers in the fish plants and those legging their way up from homelessness, built into the hillside near the only fast food outlet in town.

Gudger pointed out where the crew was building a scaffolding on top of the flat roof. The flat roof had been built in the sixties, and, with the ledge around the tarred roof, there formed an almost perfect pond that had continued to rot the ceilings of the top floor since the day it was done. Over the years various kinds of gutter arrangements had been tried, but every opening for water seemed to get plugged with either fish and shells dropped by ravens and eagles hunting in the nearby flats, or with garbage from the young people who used to drink on the roof. The most workable solution was a series of portable bilge pumps that fed a hose that drained out the back of the building into a stream that ran down the hillside to the storm drains. The tenants ate the power costs.

Gudger asked me for money twice and I told him no, even though I was carrying a case with fifty thousand dollars in it. Part of me wanted to just give it to him, but being late in the afternoon it was getting on time for Gudger's serious drinking, and he would kill himself with that much liquor, and probably several of his friends as well. I suggested he check in with the boss who was on the roof. I told him that if he raised half the money for treatment I would front him the other half. We started to part on good terms. Gudger found out his job was going to be delayed a couple of weeks because the boss was taking off on another job, then he asked me for money again, and I said no, and we still parted on good terms, with a drunkard's hug and a promise to take care. He was going to help me in getting Blossom back, Your Honors; he had simply forgotten, but I hadn't.

I knocked on Thistle's door with my right hand and the Sweeper answered.

"Fuck you, Mr. Younger. Is that my money?"

I was touched in a way, that he called me "mister," but his general appearance did not seem all that polite. He was wearing a cheap silky shirt of many neon colors, favored by Columbian cartel bosses in their mug shots. His sleeves were rolled up, and he had a dish towel in his hand. There was a gun in his belt.

"Where's my daughter?"

"She's not here. Is that my money?"

"Not that I know of."

"Don't be cute."

"I'm here for Blossom."

The Sweeper moved on the balls of his feet, his gold crucifix bouncing on his chest. Lost was his sad-sack jailbird demeanor, replaced now by the insecure energy of a small-town crook.

"Step inside," he said, and he motioned with a shrug, making me walk close to his sunken chest as I squeezed through the door. "Your daughter ran out for a bit. But she may be back soon."

I walked into the apartment. There was one light on above the stovetop in the kitchen area, and it was dark in the living room. The huge TV was on with the sound turned low: Bram Stoker's *Dracula* was playing. In the corner of the room, a teenage boy was passed out on a bean bag chair, near the oil heater. An empty pizza box with cigarette butts lay near his left arm, and garbage littered the floor: styrofoam sandwich plates, broken lighters, hamburger clamshells, four plastic vodka bottles, neon energy drink cans. A dirty dia-per lay on the linoleum floor by the bathroom door. The house smelled like excrement, mildew and stale cigarettes. On the TV, an old man savored the taste of blood from a cut on his hand.

The velour couch in front of the TV stirred with a figure, and when I looked over the back, I saw Thistle partially curled under a child's comforter, clutching her blanket with both hands like a small child. She was unconscious and naked, and her hip and buttock were exposed to the air. Her hair was stringy over her closed eyes, and her mouth was a red gash of smeared lipstick.

"You missed the party, dude," Sweeper said. He pulled out a chair near the kitchen table and sat down and looked over at another chair. "Jesus . . ." he said and jumped up and pulled a revolver from under the cushion of the chair. Saving the pistol in his belt for another occasion, I suppose. He swung the huge revolver past my face and put it on the table. I could see it was a loaded .44. "Fucking kids, man. They never pick up their shit. Am I right?"

I put the case between my feet and sat down. "We can talk about the money, but at the end of this I'm going to walk out of here with that girl and my daughter."

"Let's hope so, dude, but you better change up on your tone. We aren't in jail, and I'm not your bitch, Mr. Public Pretender."

"All right. I'm going to leave. I'm going to get Thistle dressed, and we are going to go. I'm not going to give you this case until I see Blossom."

"Fine, man. Keep it. It's yours."

"You telling me you don't want the money now? Where is Blossom? One last time."

Sweeper reached over and picked up the revolver. He pulled the hammer back and licked the end of the barrel. "She's probably out sucking dick for drugs. Am I her fucking babysitter?"

When I stood up, the chair clattered across the room. I had my right hand around his throat, and I could feel his windpipe against my palm. His pulse fluttering there like a bird, the barrel of the .44 was hard against my temple.

"Fuck you, Mr. Government Dick," Sweeper wheezed out. His gun hand was shaking. "Mr. Take a Deal, fake lawyer." His face was red and tears flicked from his eyes. "I ain't your bitch!" he said. The kid on the beanbag stirred, then rolled over, still asleep.

The gun in Sweeper's hand seemed too heavy for him now. The front rim of the barrel pressed hard into my temple, but his white fingers on the grips wove around on the end of his thin arm as if he were wringing a kitten's neck. He was confused, a hysterical child now.

"You keep the money, fuck head." He was openly crying now. His index finger was inside the trigger guard. There were no empty cylinders in the gun; lead tips caught the light in the perfectly round holes. "You keep the money and you take care of Sherrie, so she doesn't flip on me."

"You mean for Melissa Bean's disappearance?"

"For fucking anything. All you do is make people take deals. She takes a deal and keeps her mouth shut, you keep the fucking money."

Your Honors, Dashiell Hammett once wrote, "The cheaper the hood, the gaudier the patter," but in my experience, the cheaper the hood, and the more excited they are, the more frequently they use the word "fuck."

I loosened my grip and told Sweeper to take a couple of deep breaths. I told him that there was no problem so big that we had to make a "fucked for life" kind of mistake, like shooting me before I even had a chance to help him out. I used the same tone I have used when confronted by brown bears: I spoke slowly and calmly and tried to seem bigger than I was, but not challenging. With bears and with meth heads with guns, the basic rule is this: don't seem like food, and don't challenge them to a fight. Make it seem like you are just too much trouble to kill.

"Deep breath, buddy, deep breath . . . Let's walk this back a bit."

Just as he was putting the gun down, a knock came at the door. Three strong raps, then heavy footfalls on the rotten deck outside his door.

"Fuck!" he said almost smiling. He waved the gun at me like a teacher would an eraser. "Don't fucking get up."

He walked to the door and opened it a crack. I could hear him whispering. Between his legs I could see the dark shoes of a uniform and the creased blue slacks of officialdom. I could hear the creaking of leather, and then finally the squelch of a handheld radio: a woman's voice using the ten code. Sweeper was talking to a cop.

Both the cop and Sweeper were speaking in an intimate tone, almost with the breathy whisper of a young married couple about to have a whisper argument in front of their kids. Both of them were aware I was inside, both of them didn't want me to hear.

Now, Your Honors, I am not James Bond and it crossed my mind to run out the door into the arms of the police to seek their protection. But after the first two seconds of the conversation I froze in my seat, running through all of the possibilities of what was going on, and my mind kept coming up blank. The only certain impression I had was the man with the gun and the radio and his uniform shoes was not there to help me, but to help the Sweeper.

The only words I could hear from the officer, toward the end of the conversation were, "Just not here." This was spoken in a raised voice and Sweeper hushed him with words to the effect of, "Okay . . . okay." He probably said "fuck" too, but again, Your Honors, he was whispering.

"Man oh man." Sweeper shut the door and came back to me with a half-smile. "Salesmen. What you going to do?"

"Yeah . . ." there was no point of saying anything more. I went to the couch and tried to wake up Thistle. "Let's go baby," but she wouldn't rouse.

"You going to take the money?" Sweeper asked nervously. His demeanor changed. "You take it," he offered. "You do what I'm talking about. You take care of Sherrie Gault. You know what I'm saying . . ."

"I don't have any idea what you mean." I said. I left the money right where it was. I looked around in the garbage on the floor. I was not going to walk out the door with an underage drunk girl, fifty grand and a note that implicated me in a murder for hire. Nothing good would come from this money, and I was still hoping that Sweeper would take it into consideration for my daughter, wherever she was.

Near the beanbag chair was a sleeping bag with a wad of clothes jammed into the foot end. I started bundling up what looked to be Thistle's belongings and slung the girl over my shoulder

"Look, fucker . . ." Sweeper had the gun in his hand again. "You take that money and you fix this. You know what I'm saying. You can go talk with her in jail. They won't search you. You can take care of this . . ." He was stilted now, frightened, as if he were afraid of public speaking. Then it occurred to me that we were most likely being recorded, just from the way he was speaking . . . too loud and too clearly. Sweeper had indeed turned snitch.

I left the money and pulled the sleeping bag over the thirteen-year-old girl. I walked out the door with Thistle, naked in a sleeping bag.

Two officers walked up the stairs and stopped me. They searched me, disappointed, I imagine, that there was no money, no note. They grabbed the half-naked teenager and returned her to "her apartment." The one officer went in with her, stayed about five minutes while I gave his partner my information and told him that I was going to take her home to her mother. I gave the officer the number of Thistle's mom. I refused to answer any more questions about walking out of a drug house with a naked teenage girl. They threatened me with arrest for sexual assault, and I invited them to do that. They threatened me with obstruction of justice, and I invited them to do that as well, but I was not going

to talk with them about anything other than getting
Thistle to her mom or a hospital. They detained me
in cuffs and several kids in diapers peered out of
the closed curtains of another apartment down the
deck. A former client stood in pajamas in the parking lot with a beer in one hand and a cigarette in the
other. He gave me a thumbs up when they clicked
the cuffs on.

Your Honors, you may wonder why I didn't take the
money. I left it for three reasons. One: my boss told
me to take it back. Not a strong reason but a good one
none the less. Two: I suspected the cops were going to
bust me as soon as I stepped out the door, and I had no
good reason to be holding fifty grand of drug money
and carrying a drugged-up teenager in my arms. But
three and probably the most important was that it was
not my money, and I have learned that nothing good
comes of walking around with a lot of someone else's
money. Particularly if they liked to hide guns in the
cushions of their chair

I waited and said nothing. The officer came out
of Sweeper's apartment and explained that he had
spoken with Thistle and that everything "was fine"
and her mother was coming get her. The young cop
uncuffed me and told me to be careful unless I didn't
want to be given a no trespassing order from the
occupants.

They told me to leave the premises and shooed me
on my way as if I were a lost dog. The rain fell hard
enough now for the splashes in the puddles to jump

into the air: a confusion of concentric rings crisscrossed their surfaces. The mountains on the island were shrouded in flinty clouds shredding up their slopes. Water sluiced noisily down the mountain into the storm drains. I was sick to my stomach as lights blinked on around town. It was four-thirty in the afternoon.

I spent the night canvassing all of my daughter's friends by phone, and when I could not reach them, Jane Marie and I went to their houses. I still had Blossom's computer and checked her messages for clues, but my girl had gotten into the habit of erasing everything after hearing me talk about all the stupid things cops find on phones and computers they seize. I posted messages on her social media pages and emailed some of her closest friends, hoping that if I became enough of a pest to these friends and their parents, they would give her up. Jane Marie even posted a video of herself and photos of Blossom: Jane Marie smiling into the camera asking her daughter to come home with "absolutely no questions asked."

Jane Marie and I walked downtown in the rain and went to the movie theater and looked in all the rows in the flickering light, we poked into the bars and the liquor stores with her photograph, and came away with sympathetic stares and some suspicion. We went into the deserted graveyards in town and to the ends of both roads where the forest overwhelms the lights of town. There were no beach fires and no drinking parties we could find—just burned out fire pits with the ashes of shipping pallets and broken beer bottles.

I even went back to the Hillside Apartments and beat on the apartment door where the Sweeper had pulled a gun on me that day. Nothing moved behind the door: no footsteps, no television or music on. All I could hear was the stream chucking rocks down the steep hillside and the muffled sound of a radio in the apartment next door, where the older Filipino man insisted he had not seen anyone come or go all day.

Finally, we went to the police station. The dispatcher stared at us from behind the bulletproof glass. Her eyes were rimmed red and although she recognized me from my work, she did not smile.

"Yes?" she spoke from her radio console, and her voice squeezed through the slot on the bottom of the divider.

"We are here to report that our daughter is missing?" Jane Marie leaned toward the slot, trying to make a connection with the dispatcher.

"When was the last time you saw her?"

"Yesterday . . . well . . . I guess earlier today actually."

"What time? What day?" The dispatcher was not looking at us now but at the screen in front of her.

"She came by the house for some things around two o'clock P.M. of this last day."

"How old is she?"

"Thirteen."

"Do you have reason to believe that she is in imminent danger? Have you checked with her friends?"

"Yes . . . we've checked with her friends. I don't

know about imminent danger . . ." Here Jane Marie's voice began to crack and tears came to her eyes.

"I can't really file anything until she has been missing for forty-eight hours, or unless you think she is in danger." The dispatcher did not glance up from her console. She had her own cell phone sitting on her lap, and she looked down at her screen and then started texting something.

"May we speak to the lieutenant on duty?" I poked my head around Jane Marie's shoulders and into the slot. "Right away."

She looked up a bit peeved, put her cell phone down and picked up the phone next to her. "One minute . . ." she muttered.

The lieutenant was in a uniform this time, but he was not wearing a utility belt or gun. He had what looked like a gravy stain on his tie, and he wore a military-style haircut. He was carrying his reading glasses when the door to the main part of the station buzzed open, and he walked into the lobby.

"Hello, Cecil, Jane . . . come on in." We walked back toward his office. He started to go through his door, but stopped, turned back and said, "I think we would be more comfortable in here," and he showed us to the secondary interview room that they use mostly for juveniles. He offered to get us some coffee, and when we declined he said he would be right back, then left the room.

Jane Marie had tears running down her cheeks now. She trusted the police, but just being there brought on the enormity of the situation, and the fear started to grip her. "They will help us, won't they?" She snuffled and looked at me. I didn't tell her that I didn't think so. I didn't tell her that the lieutenant had put us in this room so he could video record our conversation, and he was activating the system now. I didn't tell her that the police, if they ever thought of me at all, thought only of how to put me in jail.

"So . . . what's going on tonight?" he said as he came back in with his own cup of coffee and a glass of water that he put down for Jane. The police love props. Big cops like bringing water for witnesses. I think they just like handling little flimsy paper cups because it makes them seem somehow sensitive. It wasn't working with the lieutenant; he just seemed clumsy. He looked at Jane Marie but wouldn't catch my eye at all.

I told him the entire story, beginning to end, leaving out the case of money, the dead Mexican and any implication that I had ever been asked to murder anyone or suborn perjury. I gave him the address of Sweeper and told him all about Thistle and his two patrolmen taking the drugged girl back into the apartment when I was trying to take her home. He nodded and took notes quietly and neatly: just a few words written down on a blank sheet of paper: Blossom's name and identifying numbers. Sweeper's name and address. Thistle's name and her mother's name. Times that we could remember, and at the top he wrote in thick black numbers today's time and date. He kept going back and retracing the date over and over.

"Why would she go to that apartment?" he asked Jane Marie.

"Her best friend was there . . . she is very protective of her friends." Jane Marie took a tissue from the box on the table.

"What's her experience with drugs?"

"Blossom's?"

The policeman nodded slowly.

"None, I expect."

"Is she sexually active? Do you know?" Here the lieutenant looked at me for some reason.

"No . . ." Jane Marie blurted out quickly, then, "Not to my knowledge I mean."

"We don't think so," I told him.

"Well . . ." now he started retracing the time on his paper . . . "sometimes we are the last to know, aren't we?" He smiled weakly. "Do you have a recent photo?"

Jane Marie held out her phone to him with a photograph lit up on the screen. The lieutenant glanced at it, and his eyes went down to his shoes. His shoulders hunched a bit and then he looked toward the door.

"What?" I asked him.

"How old did you say she was?"

"Thirteen." Jane Marie sensed some shift in the policeman's demeanor. "What?" she demanded. "Please tell us."

The lieutenant would not look at us. "Nothing . . ."

he said. He laid down his pen and stood up quickly. Then he sat down again.

"How old did you say she was?" he asked again without making eye contact, and before we could repeat our answer, he interrupted with another question. "And that girl our officers found you carrying out of the apartment . . . she is your daughter's best friend?"

"Yes," Jane Marie said. She sat upright and stared at the lieutenant's face, which appeared to be going pale.

"Yes . . . why?" she repeated.

"And she is . . . this girl you were carrying out of that apartment, Mr. Younger, she is older than your daughter, right?" He looked at the closed door of the interview room and then at the camera, and when he looked at the camera in the corner, his eyes widened, conscious now that he himself was being recorded.

"No, sir, she is thirteen as well," I said.

The lieutenant took all of his notes and the photograph, stood up and left the room.

"What the hell?" Jane Marie looked at me, her face now flushed with a building rage.

"I don't know, sweetie." I looked at her, genuinely confused. We sat for ten minutes. There was no sound from the hallway. I looked at the camera. Jane Marie started swearing and speculating about what was going on.

"Do you think he knows something, Cecil? Honey, is he going to come back and tell us . . . tell us something awful?"

I held her hand. I didn't want to talk in that room, and I wanted to be recorded even less than the lieutenant did. "Let's not talk about it now . . . but no, he is not going to come back and tell us something awful."

"How do you know?" she pleaded.

"Because he can't tell us what he knows. I don't think he can tell anybody."

We waited five more minutes and then got up and walked out. The dispatcher said that the lieutenant had gone out on a call. She shoved a pamphlet entitled "Straight Dope: Talking with Teens about Drugs and Personal Safety" through the slot and turned back to her console. Then we were gone.

At this point, Your Honors, I'd like to point out that I am not a young, rabid public defender. I'm not a cop hater. I generally accept that we live in a world of laws, and these laws need to be enforced. Great police work is a thing of beauty, and it has always made my job so much easier. Good, professional police work that follows the law in the letter and in the spirit is the foundation of a peaceful civilization. But that is not what happened here.

We left the police station with no more information or help than we went in with. We essentially felt that our concerns about our lost daughter had been dismissed as a personal problem and wasn't something we should be bringing to them. At least Jane Marie felt that way, and she was very upset.

I had my opinion as to what was going on and

replayed all the actions of the police as we walked home. The lieutenant was clearly not telling us what he knew. Something had scared him off . . . something that I didn't want to even guess at.

When we got home there was a message on our answering machine from the lieutenant. He sounded as if he were calling on a cell phone; there was road noise in the background. He identified himself then paused, sounding shaken as if he had received a blow. *"Listen, Cecil, we should talk, I'm sorry I had to leave back there . . . I just . . . I just . . . Listen, we need to talk, I think I can help you out."* He left his personal cell number, not the police number.

Jane Marie came back, poured herself a glass of wine and drank it straight down, then refilled her glass—extremely rare behavior for her.

"I'm going to bed. I'll have my phone by my bed, my computer too. I'm going to get up in a couple of hours and check everything again online. You know that she stays awake all night. I don't care where she is, Cecil, I swear to God"—she raised her palms above her head—"I won't complain . . . I won't criticize her . . . just as long as she comes home." At this point she started crying like a broken-hearted child. "I'm a miserable human being," she mumbled between her hands as she cried. "I'm a terrible mother and a . . . miserable human being." She sobbed.

I took her in my arms and kissed her cheeks, tasting her tears. "No, no, no . . ." I murmured as I kissed her.

"Stop that. We will find her." But even as I said it, my voice sounded hollow.

This, Your Honors, is the real beginning of the crime for which I was charged.

I left our house and walked directly to the Hillside Apartments. It was now past midnight. The streetlights cast a gauzy sheet of light in the rain, and where the light hit the black streets it refracted like broken glass. I rarely carry a gun and didn't bring one to the apartment.

The top of the Hillside Apartments was a shamble of broken scaffolding and blue plastic fiber tarps. These tarps are as useful as duct tape in our rainy climate and can be used for wrapping everything you want to keep dry, from houses and boats to stacks of firewood. In Ketchikan, not too long ago, two bodies were found in blue tarps within a year. The city assembly considered requiring a three-day waiting period to buy them; but it never got past the first reading. On the flat roof of the Hillside, the tarps were stitched together and had collapsed in on the scaffolding like the shrunken carcass of a large ungulate, desiccated somewhere on the plains. Edges fluttered in the wind and in the center of the roof, rain was gathering into a comfortably sized pond.

Sweeper's apartment still had the curtains drawn. There was no evidence of lights or noise, but two doors down the low sound of music and the babble of voices rose above the sound of rainfall. I stood for a few seconds at the door and listened: men talking and the clicking of chips on a felt table. I walked in.

Five men sat at a round table under a low hanging light. The edges of the room were in shadow. The men sat in front of a stack of chips, three white men and two older Filipinos. Two of the white men had big guts and smoked cigars, the other white man seemed fit and wore a visor with sunglasses. The two Filipinos wore expensive-looking football jerseys: one from the Seahawks, the other the Raiders. They were smoking cigarettes and each of them had gold rings on both hands and one had a gold nugget watchband. The players did not look at me, but a very large Tongan man, whom I knew from the Public Defender Agency, stepped directly in front of me and put his hand on my chest.

"No, Mr. Younger . . . this is invitation only. You been invited?"

"Ike, I'm just here looking for two girls."

With that the white men laughed. "Who isn't buddy?" one of them said softly.

"Emily and Blossom. Thirteen-year-old girls. Where are they?"

A fat man threw in a pile of chips and said, "I'll see you and raise five hundred."

Then Sweeper stepped forward and ducked his head into the circle of light above the table. "Sit down, Cecil. Have a drink."

A fat man blew smoke from his cigar. "Two thirteen-year-olds? You don't want much, do you, buddy?" I knew the white men from around town: a contractor, a retired postman, and a pilot. The Filipinos I only knew from seeing them on the street. The older Filipinos in Sitka mostly stay clear of the criminal courts. Gambling is their usual vice, and it followed rules that did not need to be enforced by the government.

"Where is she?"

"Sit. Drink. I'll get you in the game a little later," Sweeper said.

A hand with the force of gravity pushed me into a chair. In the darkness were two doors. One of them opened a crack and the head of a child peeked out. I started to get up, and Ike pushed me down again.

"Sit, Cecil." He put a glass of whiskey with ice in my hand.

"You don't drink, do you?" Sweeper said.

"Not in a long time."

"Your girls ever seen you drink?"

"No."

The door stayed open a second and two heads stood in the doorway.

"Drink that," Sweeper said. "I'll go get her."

I looked at the whiskey in the glass; I set it on the floor.

"Drink it, you superior son of a bitch. Drink it, Mr. Public Pretender," he snarled, and I heard the fury of every condescending thing I had ever said to him. The deals he swallowed when his memory was blacked out, the fake concern in my voice when I had asked him to go into treatment. His rage was deep and black and well-founded. "Drink it, Mr. Perfect."

And I did. My first taste of alcohol in almost thirty

years. My stomach tightened wanting to refuse it, then it blossomed in my guts as the steam rose into my head. I drank the entire glass down in one gesture.

I hate to admit it, Your Honors, because it sounds so cliché, but within thirty seconds of having that one drink I felt all the old feelings of deep thirst come back to me. The drunk inside of me woke up like Snow White. I was thirty years younger and completely absorbed in the flavor and the buzz of the whiskey.

I drank another glass that Ike poured for me, and all the self-loathing I had ever felt came rushing through my body. Ego, disease, and self-pity: all my failures were right there in the forefront of my mind, and it made me thirsty. As if I had forgotten it, I realized that I was a drunk and had always been one. Why had I tried to deny it during all these miserable years of sobriety? I asked for another, but Ike told me to slow down.

A fat man slapped down his cards, "I'm out, God damn it." He pushed his chair back from the table. "Get me one of those sandwiches," he called over his shoulder. I heard a refrigerator door open, and a harsh light sliced through the room from the corner. A girl, not more than ten years old, wearing a silky top and short shorts, came out of the darkness carrying a plate with a fat sandwich and a bag of chips.

"And a beer," the fat man said. The girl squinted into the bright light and skipped back into the darkness. I heard ice rustling in a cooler, and she danced back to the fat man with a sweating long-necked bottle.

"Thank you, darlin'. Come sit with me and change my luck."

The girl crawled up on his lap and curled her head into the hollow of his neck.

"Good, sweet girl," he said and patted her on the leg. He took a bite of the sandwich and a tongue of rare roast beef flopped out of the bread and hung on his lip. He popped it between his teeth with one finger, then kissed the girl's shoulder leaving a smear of mustard on her skin. She made a face, then wiped the mustard off with her wrist, as if she were being drooled on by a puppy.

The unlucky one slapped his cards down. "The heck with this, Harold, if you aren't playing, how am I going to get my money back? I'm going to change my luck a little, while you enjoy your snack." The others chuckled. He stood up, walked to the first door and opened it to reveal a well-lit room. There were posters on the walls, and pop music played on a small stereo. In silhouette in the doorway stood Thistle, wearing her pajamas. Behind her on the bed was someone else covered by a blanket. The unlucky one had his back to the darkness and began to walk into the light.

From this point on, Your Honors, I will admit the details are hazy and somewhat jumbled. I remember clearly standing up and punching Ike, with little or no effect. I remember the door knocking, people shuffling around and grabbing for their chips. Sweeper stood by a small floor safe with his handgun drawn. Ike struck me in the face, and I hit flat on the floor by the card table right on my ass as if I were going to sit in a chair but missed. I seem to remember the lieutenant walking into the room. He was wearing a Hawaiian shirt. He was angry and kept asking, "What is he doing here?" I remember him saying something like, "Get him out of here now. Get them all out of here. Jesus Christ."

I crawled under the table and made a lunge for the bedroom door, but someone grabbed me. I could feel strong fingers digging into my forearms. Then someone punched me so hard in the stomach that I lost all my wind and probably some whiskey. Then I was pulled up again, got another blow to my face, and I blacked out.

An unspecified later time, the darkness was cooling, and I still felt the love-hatred of whiskey drifting in my skull. I was numb . . . sad, I remember that . . . and then came the pain of waking up and my deep, abiding thirst.

At first I didn't recognize where I was. I was on the floor of an ordinary room, and the carpet had a chemical smell. First, I saw shoes, expensive leather shoes, on a man sitting in a chair. I tried to raise my head to see something more than an ankle, but I was only able to focus on a stain on the carpet. Under the bite of the chemical cleaner I could smell the rotten meat-package smell of blood.

"Mr. Younger . . . what are you doing here?" The

man's voice was pinched and deep, yet I could tell he was carrying more than a little sarcasm around with him.

I rolled over and stared up at the ceiling. There was a hint of brownish-red spots . . . high-velocity blood spatter that the cleaners had missed. I wanted to throw up, but I choked it down, not knowing who I was dealing with yet.

"I'll leave in a second," I said straight into the air.

"Take it easy . . . You will need a few minutes to get your legs under you. You took a good hit." I recognized the voice but couldn't place it. I turned over on an elbow and looked at the man in the chair.

"You know me, right?"

I did; it was Wynn Sanders, the man who both owned a large share of the fish plant and the hotel, whose carpet I was about to foul.

"It's been a while since we saw each other at a Rotary lunch, Younger."

"No, sir," I managed, "I saw you the other day when I was going into the hotel. You were cleaning the sidewalk."

"No," he said, "You must be mistaken, sir. I never saw you out front of my hotel. Not that day or any other day."

Now, Your Honors, even in a post-truth America, I knew this guy was lying, and I knew that he was not going to admit to being at that hotel when the Mexican Mule was put down.

"Once you manage to get up, I'll take you to see

something," he said. I sat up and stared at him. The left side of my face was swollen and there was a ringing in my ears. Mr. Sanders was coming in and out of focus. I looked at him, trying to make sense of my circumstances. The first thing that I was realizing was that I was in the same hotel room where the Mexican Mule had been shot. I recognized the smell and the blood spatter, no matter that someone had made an attempt to clean it.

"Hey. Where the hell is my daughter?" I asked.

"Ah, children . . ." he said and stood up. He offered his hand to help me stand, but I lumbered to my feet without his help. "They will break your heart, won't they? Come on, walk with me."

I followed him down the hall. The floors seemed soft and yet, my head ached with each step. We left the room and went down a maze of halls and stairwells.

"You should be asking what happened to *my* daughter, Younger."

"I'm sorry about your girl. I really am, but where is Blossom?" Now my voice was echoing off hard concrete.

Mr. Younger . . . you work hard. I know you do. I've watched you and your African boss. You and he put in your hours but still, you caused her death."

"No," I said, "we did not. She died from her addiction."

"Government workers, always so politically correct . . . I knew I should have gotten, how do they say it in the jail? A real lawyer, but back then I thought I was going to teach her a lesson . . . my God, what a damnable mistake that was." He turned at the top of the stairway and looked at me. Muscles in his jaw were flexing, and blood vessels on his temple bulged blue. "I truly hate political correctness, it's the cowardly proselytizing of the liberal elite, the naïve and the out of touch."

I stared at him for a moment. He wore a blue sports coat and checked shirt. No tie. He had tan slacks. He had a shoulder holster and a semi-automatic of some kind tucked under his arm. In Alaska, you can carry a concealed weapon without a permit or so much as a "by your leave." More than half the men in the grocery store are packing a gun, in case they might need to kill someone in the produce section, so the gun didn't worry me that much. What worried me more was the large ring of keys he carried and the number of stairs we were descending. I felt sure we were going someplace with many locks, someplace hardened and secure. The lights became more and more dim as we went down another staircase, as if we were heading into a dungeon.

"You probably don't even know that you are working for the death merchants, do you? You tell yourself you are protecting the underclass, but you are allowing them to die . . . or rot in prison."

"And what is it you are doing?" I asked.

"Before you start in on me with your politically correct judgments, let me just ask you if you have ever had the need for revenge," he said.

"Come on, really?" I said.

"You know drug people."

"Yes I do. If they are addicted they have no choice but to get more drugs."

"My Lord, Mr. Younger . . . I should just shoot you right now." His voice echoed up the stairwell like a pool ball bouncing down the steps.

"All your liberal understanding . . . none of it is saved for the aggrieved," he said.

I stopped and leaned against the wall. "Where is Blossom?"

"Of course you are concerned." He opened the last heavy metal door.

Inside was a full-scale industrial laboratory, complete with safety posters and eye-wash stations. Industrial lights hung from the concrete ceiling in cages. Three men in matching coveralls and safety goggles were walking around the tanks. Two of them seemed to be cleaning up, and the other was making notes next to an industrial scale and a stack of white buckets. Each bucket was sealed and marked as fish oil, but lying out on the table were trays of glassy crystals.

"Teach a man to fish and he'll have food forever," he swung his arm as if he were unveiling a new car.

"So making huge profits off the industry that killed your daughter is your idea of revenge?"

"You know drug people. You know the people who got her addicted, and the people who killed her. Once I was making the product they desired most in the world, I owned them. They come to me for everything. They are absolutely mine, and now all of them, including you, are disposable widgets. Soon I will have all of their money, and their reputations"—he stopped and stared at me a moment—"and all of them will be dead. This is the best revenge, and it's something to which I am suited."

"All right. Fine. but what am I doing here? Am I just getting a tour of your drug lab?"

"Oh, but there is much more." Sanders walked toward the far side and opened another door and flipped on the lights. There in the middle of the room were six pallets stacked four by four feet high with boxes wrapped tightly in sheets of plastic, and around the walls were racks of guns hanging on punch board hooks: black assault rifles and handguns.

He laid one hand reverently on top of the wrapping on one of the pallets. "Have you ever wondered what half a million rounds of ammunition looks like?" he asked me, and all I did was shake my ringing head.

"I can tell you this, but no one else. Someone very close to me killed that Mexican on that day you didn't see me . . . and here we have my supply of ammunition to take care of everyone else: .308, .222, nine-millimeter and, of course, a great deal of .22 long rifle hollow points." I stared at him as he petted the pile of ammunition as if it were a long-haired cat.

"You must be a bad shot," I said finally.

"Funny," and he turned away. "Are you Jewish, Younger?"

"What does that have to do with anything?" I stared at him in the metallic shadow. Then I added, "But no, I am not Jewish."

"But you don't mind serving the Jews, do you?"

"Oh my Lord, Sanders. Really?"

"Really . . . the media, television, radio, banking, the court system . . . all of them are Jewish enterprises, designed to keep them in their internationalist leadership roles. You don't mind having your culture and heritage controlled by the alien cultures?"

"There are like twenty-five Jews in Sitka. How can you work up any hate at all? Jesus Christ, Sanders."

He chuckled. "For a social justice warrior you aren't very 'big picture,' are you, Mr. Younger. You have no idea of the forces at work."

"I guess not." I attempted to hold him in focus, and tried not to spit my words at him. "You know people hate Nazis. I'm not making that up. You can Google it." I was still weak and leaned against the column of ammunition. "I mean, do you have *any* friends?" My cogent rhetoric was not winning the day apparently.

"You are a snob, aren't you? Like all your kind, you hold on to your intellectual superiority as if it were . . ." and here he paused to smile at some joke . . . "bullet-proof."

"Were you bullied as a child? Did the kids with glasses tease you on the playground?" I said.

"I'm just an investor . . . like Kennedy, like Gates," he said. He walked toward the far corner of his bunker. "I'm investing in the coming war against the government. I make something that people want, and I'm investing in the most conservative commodity there is . . . Cecil . . . I'm going to call you that . . . I invest in the oldest commerce there is."

"Shut up. Please, just stop."

"Tools of death, Cecil . . . They are a sure thing."

"You're an idiot."

"Okay . . . but I have personal freedom. I have more than you and your Jewish bigots. You know it, and Sherrie, your client, knows it." He paused, waiting for me to take his meaning, but I was looking at the guns, wondering if they were loaded and if I could use one of them on him.

"I have something else to show you," he said, and I think he was disappointed I didn't want to talk politics with him anymore.

He turned to his right and under a single lamp lay a large bundle wrapped in a green tarp, trussed up with groundline The only thing it looked like to me was a body. Mr. Sanders took a knife from his pocket and tore open the top section. He rolled the body to the left and made a circular hole in the tarp. The bundle flopped to one side and there, staring through the hole, was the shattered mouth and the misshapen face of the police lieutenant. He still wore his Hawaiian shirt. His lips were stippled black from gunpowder, and his teeth were shattered. His face was blue-black from massive bruising, and the back of his head appeared to be missing.

"Killed himself, can you believe it?"

"He did this to himself?"

"Oh yes, Cecil . . . he was distraught about his sex life. Terribly depressed."

"Really . . ." I said slowly as I worked to keep my stomach down.

"I'm not a liar, Cecil . . . He found out he had had sex with an underage girl at one of the card games. Thirteen years old . . . can you believe it?"

I looked down at the police lieutenant's body. The mouth was wide and dark, his eyes open in an expression of otherworldly panic.

"What's he doing here?" I said slowly.

"We were in the middle of a discussion about how I could help him, when he pulled his service weapon and"—Sanders leaned back down and covered the misshapen face—"then he did this. Sad, really."

"How were you going to help him?"

Wynn Sanders knocked on the door to the bunker. Sweeper walked in leading Thistle by the arm. She was in nothing but her bra and panties. She walked awkwardly, as if she were more mannequin than girl. She saw me, but only a slight flicker of recognition registered on her face.

"He refused to do what you are now going to do for me."

"Let her go . . ." I whispered.

"Hold on now. Please, be patient, son."

"Hey, Mr. Y . . ." the dazed girl slurred. Sweeper tossed her against the pile of ammunition.

"You should know that I have your daughter. She is safe and healthy. You need to remember this before you do anything foolish."

I walked toward Thistle and took her soft small hand. "Let's go," I told her.

"Wait, wait, wait . . . hold your horses," Sanders said

in a playful voice. "I want you to kill Sherrie Gault in the jail. You have to do it before tomorrow at six P.M."

"You can't be serious."

"I am . . . you were not my first choice, believe me, but"—he shrugged at the body of the lieutenant—"things change . . . It's dynamic. I'm kind of spitballing here."

I looked around and thought of the lab, with its deep sinks, stainless tables and work spaces. "You killed that missing girl . . . you killed Melissa Bean."

"That is not your problem, and, by the way, no, I didn't kill her, she died from natural causes, but you know how corrupt the court system is . .."

I looked at Sweeper and spoke straight to my former client, "You were going to turn this guy over. You were going to send him to jail . . ."

"Shut the fuck up, Pretender." Sweeper spit his words at me as if they were acid in his mouth.

"You are going to do this for me, Cecil. You are going to kill Sherrie in the jail before she can give a statement and before she is flown out to Juneau for safe keeping."

"You can't be serious. I can't do that."

"Look at something for me." He nodded to Sweeper, who produced a color photograph printed out on regular paper. He held it to my face. It was a picture of the naked body of my daughter, with her hands bound behind her back. The look in her eyes was nothing like Thistle's dulled expression as she looked up at me from the floor. In the photo, Blossom's eyes were awake and filled with terror. She was sober and alive . . . struggling to free herself.

"If the cops transport Sherrie Gault . . . if she gets on that jet to Juneau in handcuffs, I'm going to shoot your daughter. I'll shoot her as soon as the plane leaves the ground."

"How can you do that to these children?" I said. My voice was breaking now.

He looked at me with a kind of pity and said, "In this, I feel nothing. There are no more innocents. You will feel the same way after your daughter is gone."

"You cannot do this . . ." I said, pleading openly now and trying to move to Thistle as the Sweeper pushed me back.

"Actually, I can. It's easy. You see, this is the way I motivate people. Come on now, son, just watch." Sanders pushed me in the corner away from the girl. Then in one smooth motion Sweeper weakly gestured toward Thistle, then pulled out his gun and shot her in the back of the head with a single, ringing pop.

I fell to the floor. I remember screaming, or rather making random open-mouthed sounds. I reached her, and her muscles twitched in my arms. She shook violently twice and was done.

"I know this hurts, son. I really do, but you now work for me." Sanders said and his voice floated in the room.

"By tomorrow at six p.m. If Sherrie Gault leaves this island, your daughter dies just like her friend here. Do you have any doubt that I will win this game?" he whispered in my ear.

Then, I was up on the street. Someone had cleaned my hands and taken my shirt off. I was wearing only my jacket, and the rain was falling as icy tears. The next thing I did, Your Honors, is not something I'm proud of and in retrospect was a serious mistake, but I walked across the street and bought a warm quart of whiskey and drank it as quickly as I could.

Drinking the whiskey caused me to lose three hours of my twenty-seven. It was six-thirty when I walked into my house. I held on to the banister with both hands and lurched up the stairs. At the landing, Jane Marie was standing with tears running down onto her cheeks. She looked at me and stepped forward to smell my breath.

"Oh my God!" she said and then covered her eyes. "Are you kidding me . . . Our daughter is missing. You disappear and give me no information where you fucking disappear to, and then you turn up drunk? Unbelievable."

I walked to the kitchen and poured a cup of cold coffee and retched in the sink. I drank the coffee down in five gulps then fully threw up. I had less than twenty-four hours to murder my client or find my girl, whichever came first.

"Sorry," I said trying to flick the black stains off my shirtfront.

"The police won't answer my calls. Her friends are frantically trying to find her. Todd is walking around town and just calling her name as if she were a lost dog . . . and where the hell are you?" Jane Marie's voice was leaden and accusatory.

"I went to a card game to get her back." I said . . . or at least I think I said. What was certain was Jane Marie threw a dry shirt at me and held out a clean denim jacket. She jammed some loose bills into the jacket pocket and started punching me.

"Get out of my house." She was shrill now. "Get out and don't come back. Go."

I may have fallen down the staircase because I was bleeding when I veered out onto Katlian Street in the rain. I went back to the liquor store and bought another bottle. The woman didn't want to serve me but had no good reason not to; she only shook her head sadly as she handed me the sack.

I went up and into the woods alongside the waterfront, then into the old graveyard. I was looking for a friend, a friend who communed with spirits.

Your Honors, I know over the years you have come upon people who claimed to have committed crimes when they were in a state of drunken blackout. They assert that they did not commit a crime of specific intent because they were too drunk to form a coherent intention. I am not going to assert that, for I feel that a drunkard's mind is a very fragile and leaky vessel. Memories lie sprinkled on the neural pathways like mushrooms, and like mushrooms those memories have shallow roots. One bump or misstep may sever a memory from the ground. That is only to say that most alcoholic blackouts are the convenient work of the subconscious protecting the drunkard from himself. I believe we forget what we want to forget. If we forget slapping our wife, it's because the alcohol is protecting us from her glittering, accusatory eyes. If we forget whether the other guy had a knife in his hand before stabbing him, it is only alcohol protecting us from that look of horror as the knife squishes through the fat and finds bone. Alcohol is a narcissist's fuel . . . and, Your Honors . . . all drunkards are narcissists. This is what I honestly believe and not a plea for pity, for pity is a drunkard's oxygen. I need neither now.

I wandered through the gloomy woods where the rain drops grew fat as they fell through the canopy of limbs, and the fat devil's club leaves nodded as if in agreement as they were battered by the rain. The ground was a quilt of moss and root wads. Wind was sighing in the shadow as I stumbled around looking for Gudger Whelks.

Homeless people can camp on public land three days and then the police move them on. Some couch surf through friends' and relatives' homes, others pack up their gear and find different spots to pitch their woeful tents in the rain. On this day, the graveyard was an encampment of people crowded under tarps and rain flys. Small fires burned under tarps, and candles flickered inside the flimsy tents: gauzy mushrooms of light in the forest. Smoke drifted among the toppled graves. As I broke through the brush, former clients stood and watched me wobbling toward them. There was Binky and Rex, who had been jailed on several occasions for assaulting each other. There was CoCo, who had stabbed her husband so many times the boys in the ER called him "Zipper." There was Alex, who had once walked into the police station with a foot of his own intestine in his hands. He gave me a big loose-limbed wave. Children ran around a fire, and somewhere in a dark tent a baby was crying. Bags of food hung in trees, and ravens sat on the limbs trying to pierce the bags with their beaks.

Alex came up to me and reached for the bottle. "You on vacation, Cecil?"

"I'm looking for Gudger," I said.

Alex took a drink and pointed down the hill.

I stumbled down the mossy hillside and tried to adjust my eyes to the darkness. Finally, I sighted a brown tarp in the northern corner, where the old wooden crosses and marble slabs lay crooked in the ground. Under the tarp was a light, and that light was attached to Gudger's head.

"Here . . ." I said as I gave him the bottle. "I'm sorry I've been such an asshole."

Gudger looked at me at first as if I were a ghost who had just stumbled in to camp, but when his fingers felt the cool glass of the unmistakable whiskey jug in the wet bag, he smiled.

"You still got that job on the Hillside Apartments?" I asked him as he twisted the whiskey cap off and threw it away.

"Kind of." Gudger leaned away from me, protecting what was his bottle now. "The foreman took off. I'm just supposed to keep an eye on the scaffolding and make sure the tarps are good and the decking on the roof doesn't get wet."

"Good . . ." I said and ripped the bottle away from him and took my own deep slug. "I need you to go to work tomorrow morning."

"What you talking about?" Gudger said, his face already turning into the drunkard's slack mask.

I held up the bottle and waved it in front of his eyes. "I need you to go to work tomorrow," I said again.

"Hell, yeah." Gudger said, and he gently took the bottle back and drank as if he were coming out of the desert. I curled under the tarp and drank with him until the bottle was gone. We drank quickly because news of the bottle had reached others, and they were beginning to totter down the hill like zombies. The fat drops pattered down on the tarp like kernels of corn. I rolled closer to Gudger so he could hear me over the din. We drank and talked about what needed to be done. I might have slept. I might have dreamed of flying over town, only to swoop down and pick Blossom up into my arms, but I'm not sure.

It was a sickly gray dawn in the graveyard when I walked out. I drank a cup of tea with CoCo around her fire. I ate a damp sweet roll and a piece of bacon. I was drunk enough to be foolish, but not drunk enough to burn with the anger I was going to need. I needed an untraceable gun and some methamphetamine. I went looking for Robert Boomer. I had twelve hours, but I also had a plan to stop the clock.

The trailer house was down the road. It was a single-wide with a built-on porch. The room was thick with moss, and the wrinkled siding was streaked with mildew. Dog shit dotted the mud in the beaten-down area where the village pitbull-rat-dog hybrid pulled on his chain. An old Johnson outboard motor sat on a rack with the lower unit in a garbage can of water. The water looked black with oil, and the power head was sprung open, its clockwork guts spilling out. Raindrops rippled the dark water on the surface of the can. On the way there I had bought a new bottle and was drinking it from a bag. My clothes were muddy and soaked through. My mousey gray hair streaked down my skull. The windows of the single-wide were lined with blankets to keep the summer sun out, even though it was now fall. I didn't knock but walked right in. Music played from a single speaker in the darkness. The only chairs were broken and laying like dead horses on their sides. Figures flopped in sleeping bags in the corner, and a coffee maker burbled on the counter.

Suddenly, Mr. Boomer appeared silhouetted in a lit doorway. His overalls were unbuttoned, and they drooped over his gut. His dirty sweatshirt was stained with either taco or spaghetti sauce.

"Cecil . . . what the fuck man?" He rubbed his hand over the stubble of his hair.

"I need something to keep me going."

"Dude . . . you're drunk." He walked over to the kitchen area and clipped up one strap of his overalls.

"Have some coffee." He pulled a mug out of a cabinet, poured black coffee and righted a chair. "Here.
Sit, please," he said, and he held his hand out like a
headwaiter.

I sat down and took the cup. The coffee was hot
and strong. As I sipped it a tiny sparkler of fear was lit
in my stomach. I was beginning to feel the outriders
of normalcy . . . or reasonableness . . . and with that I
started to fear I was going to lose my resolve.

Your Honors, Mario Andretti once said, "If everything seems under control you're just not going fast
enough." I had to go fast. Mr. Boomer and I talked
about what needed to be done. He gave me some
meth, and we smoked it, and I told him I needed him
to build me a bomb in three hours maximum. He
didn't have an untraceable gun, but he knew a guy
who might lend me one.

The meth split my drunkard's head open like a
lightning bolt for a few moments. My heart raced and
the fog lifted. The day seemed clear as gin for a few
moments more. Then the chemical buzz faded like the
chiming of a bell. It didn't last as long as I needed, but
the residue of the chemical thrill in my head gave me
enough false courage to go to a cabin to find a gun.

Robert Boomer took me there and made an intro-
duction. The cabin was Spartan: twelve by sixteen
perhaps with a camp stove, a lantern, a table and a
cot. Under the cot was a GI-issue green footlocker
and some ammo boxes with yellow lettering. My man
in the cabin wore nicely patched jeans and a thermal

long undershirt. Everything was tidy; nothing was out of place. My man had wet and neatly combed black hair and he had shaved his sideburns so high they showed the boney white of his scalp. He seemed jumpy sharing his cabin space with the two of us. He kept walking to the corners of his one room as if he were a bobcat in a large crate. He didn't ask any questions when Robert broached the subject of borrowing a handgun for the day. He just reached down, then slid out his footlocker, positioning it so the open lid blocked the contents. He took out three old-looking revolvers; one with a long barrel like a cowboy gun, one medium like an old service revolver and the other was a pug-nosed wheel gun the kids liked to call a Bulldog: very large caliber, not accurate for any kind of long-range shooting. This was a Jack Ruby gun for shoving into someone's guts and pulling the trigger. It would carve out a hole in a man.

I took the Bulldog and told him I would return it. The only thing he said to me that gave me any sense of knowing was, "No need to return it if it's too much trouble," and he stressed the last three words. He gave me a handful of shells and Robert thanked him before he turned to go. My man turned to follow, and I looked down at the outside of the footlocker, where stylized twin *S*'s of the Nazi storm troopers were stenciled. Then I noticed he had the numeral *88* tattooed on the top of his right wrist.

"Is he a close friend of yours?" I asked Mr. Boomer as we walked down the road to his trailer.

"Naw, man, he's just a guy. Don't worry about it."

"Are there lots of Nazis in town?"

"Ah . . . Cecil that guy's not a Nazi. You know, he's just a history buff is all."

"Why'd he give me the gun?"

"Ah . . . well, I guess he just likes to know they are being used."

I clambered up into the woods. Gudger was still asleep under the tarp. I had stopped off at the dime store and bought him a notebook and a pen. I rousted him awake. There was three-quarters of an inch of whiskey in the bottom of the bottle, and I finished it. Gudger looked sadly at the empty as if it had betrayed him as he rose from his damp bower under the tarp. The rain had eased to a heavy mist under the canopy of trees. We walked to the bar, and I bought coffee for the two of us and a shot for Gudger to steady his hand. I handed him the notebook and pen.

"Here you go, just like I said . . . Now tell me what we talked about last night?"

"I'm going to work?" His expression seemed as if he were pleading with me.

"What are you going to do there, Gudge?"

"Man . . . I don't know . . . give me another drink."

I ordered three more. The bartender set them down and walked away quickly.

"You are going to tell all the tenants at the Hill-side that you need to look into each room to check for water leaks. It has to do with the roof repair." I drank a shot and the whiskey blossomed in my head. My hands were shaking, maybe from the meth, maybe just from my life and the fact that my clothes were soaked through again with the constant rain.

"I'm going to go into each room looking for your daughter . . . and tell you where she is." He nodded, then brushed the tendrils of his wet hair back off his face, and he took a deep breath as if psyching himself up. He tried to open his eyes wide. He downed another shot and his eyes watered. "Another . . ." he said, and I ordered two more. I was beginning to feel the pain of what I was about to do. I tore the photo of Blossom I had grabbed from the meth lab, so that Gudger would remember what her face looked like. I couldn't bear to give him the full picture of our naked girl. As I handed it to him it looked as if I were fanning myself with it, my hands shook so hard. Gudger's hands were shaking as well. We needed something else in our chemical mix.

Down the bar, the morning coffee clutch of old men and hard drinkers was discussing the militia movement, and one of them was talking about how much firepower it took to pierce a Kevlar vest.

"Those guys don't make it easy . . . got to make the head shots work," said one.

Your Honors, have you ever learned a new word in the morning and then noticed that somehow you come across that word several times in the same afternoon? It makes me wonder how much I'm missing, how much I might not understand in my day-to-day walking around. Had I been living in a little town honeycombed with right wing seditionists all my adult life and simply not understood it until this very moment? Or was I just drunk again, and maybe jacked up on some meth? One of the old men at the end of the bar was a former client. I told him I needed something to sober us up.

He smiled and we walked into the ally to snort a line of flake cocaine off the hollows where his thumb met his wrists. He fronted it to us, knowing I would be back to buy more. He turned and watched a police car cruise north on Katlian street and snickered. "Fucking doughnut eaters."

I thanked him for the cocaine and told him I would be back. Gudger had the glittering eyes of a bobcat by the time I walked him to the Hillside, and he went in carrying his paper and pencil out in front of him as if it were a trick-or-treat bag.

If they transported Sherrie at six o'clock I had eight hours before Sanders's deadline. I stuck the SS man's gun in my belt at the small of my back, walked up over the small hill to the grocery store, made a quick stop and then went down to the side of the State building where the police department sat behind the tan concrete of its seventies-style "house of the future" architecture.

At the convenience store I bought some mouthwash and deodorant. They didn't have combs or a tooth brush. They did have cologne but I didn't buy any. No cologne, because too much cologne is not only obnoxious, it draws attention to your condition. There is a small section in *Baby's First Felony* dedicated to covering up your smell: dos and don'ts. The smell on your breath after drinking is not alcohol but the chemical byproduct of your body's burning the alcohol up. It smells like flowery acetone. The flavoring in the booze gives it the weird flowery smell. So, perfume or cologne usually increases the smell of what we associate with booze on the breath. Coffee and cigarettes can mask it with just the usual bad breath. But still, terrible breath draws unwanted attention. The best is a good scrubbing of the teeth and tongue, a change of clothes and maybe a couple of sticks of gum.

I went to the thrift store and walked out back where people drop off donations. I found a clean shirt that fit. Wet pants were acceptable in Sitka. Everyone had wet pants. Then I ducked into the drugstore and bought some peppermints, a tooth brush, a cheap comb, and a travel tube of tooth paste. I brushed my teeth under a broken gutter where a stream of fresh water was spattering into the street. So by the time I showed up at the jail, the jailer on duty ignored the wet clothes and barely gave me a sniff. Taped to the glass window of the dispatcher's cage was a flyer offering twenty-five thousand dollars for information leading to the location of Melissa Bean.

"Any knives, guns, nuclear weapons?" the jailer asked and lazily waved her metal detector wand in the air about a foot away from me.

"Not this time, Betty," I said. She turned and walked me down to the interview room, where she had Sherrie Gault chained to the wall. Betty was used to me showing up unannounced, and as long as I didn't mess with her meal or court schedule she was cool with me, so I made a point to thank her. She looked over her shoulder as she was cuffing Sherrie up and told me that she was going to be fingerprinting a couple of forest service employees back in the booking room, so that when I was done just "leave her there, and I'll come get her when I can," and she nodded to Sherrie. I said I would slip out the back door, which is about twelve feet from the interview room. It opens up onto the parking lot, where I could bolt out and down to the harbor and get into a skiff perhaps a block away. From there I could get out into the Gulf of Alaska in minutes. I had no idea what I would do next, not to mention that the entire spectacle, every move I made from inside the interview room through the parking lot and into the harbor, would be covered by security cameras.

I sat down under the clock where the camera lens was secreted. If the cops could see anything at all it was only my feet. I sat down softly so the gun didn't tap against the plastic seat.

"You okay Cecil?" Betty asked, "Looks like your back's a little tender." She eyed how I was sitting with my back straight and nearer the edge of the chair.

"Soft mattress, Betty, I'm trying to talk Jane Marie into a new one, but you know her . . . She's putting the money into boat gas."

"Yeah . . . Don't worry your pretty little head about it, Cecil. Just buy the damn thing. Nothing is more important than a good night's sleep."

"Yeah . . ." was all I said.

"Yeah . . ." she repeated and watched me for a beat longer than I was comfortable. I stretched my back, made a face and Betty closed the door.

Sherrie Gault looked at me through sleepy eyes. Her clean hair was rumpled in front of her face. "What have you found out?" She yawned as she spoke to me.

"Your boyfriend is a dick." My hands were shaking and I felt like a bobblehead doll.

"Wow . . . really?"

"He pimps little girls to policemen in order to blackmail them, and when he is done with the girls, he shoots them in the head."

"That sounds like him." She barely opened her eyes. "But what about my case?"

"What did you do to piss off Wynn Sanders?"

"What about my case?"

I reached behind me and took the ugly little gun from my belt. "Sanders wants me to execute you, before you rat him out for the killing of Melissa Bean."

Her eyes widened a bit, but not in fear. "You planning on spending his money in the prison commissary?" She looked around our little room in the middle of the police station. "That's a hell of a lot of shampoo," she added.

I pulled the Bulldog's stubby hammer back. "He's got my daughter." Now her eyes brightened with something like concern.

"Wait . . ." she said and closed her eyes, thinking . . . thinking. "Sanders is *such* an asshole," was all she came up with.

"Tell me about it."

She brushed her hair off her face with her free hand and tried tucking it behind her ears. She leaned back as if she were smoking a cigarette. "We used to sell the Mexican crank. The Mexicans are using Sitka and the cold storage for their main Alaskan drop point. They have guys on boats bringing the dope up. They have tables set up on the back deck of a crab boat where they sew the dope into the bellies of the salmon. Looks weird as hell. I guess they bought the crabber because they saw it on TV and thought it looked cool. They unload the salmon onto other boats and they unload it to the cold storage, and it all looks like the fish business. They ship money back the same way and only air freight to restaurants, which gets picked up by kitchen crews or truck drivers. It's nice. We were just selling to keep ourselves in supply. Then it got bigger, the money got too good, but then my shitty little boyfriend got into taking the dope all the time. His judgment went out the fucking window."

"Short trip," I said. I put the gun back in my coat pocket, the hammer still cocked. "Speaking of out the window, was it your friend who killed the Mexican Mule?"

"I'm getting there," she snapped. "You know how these Mexicans have a jillion different jobs?"

"Yeah, hardworking bastards."

"Well one of these little bastards worked both in the fish plant and at one of Sanders's restaurants, and he starts yapping to one of his buddies about the meth business and Sanders gets wind of it. Then he wants in. He comes to us wanting to buy a shitload, and we sell him some. Then a cop comes and shakes us down, threatens to put us away for like, ten years. The cop tells us to get out of the business, and Sanders steps forward with a plan to get the cops off our back. So . . ."

"You end up working for him," I help her.

"Yes. Sanders gets the prettiest girls he can find to start slinging. He calls them his 'angels.' Fuck, what an asshole."

"Okay," I offered through the electric sludge of my perceptions.

"He knows about the card game because he owns the building, the Hillside. So, he takes over the card game and starts bringing girls in."

"Young girls?" my hand tightened around the Bull-dog's grips.

"Not at first. In the beginning it was just the regular old drug hoes."

"Melissa Bean?"

"She was sweet in the beginning. She wasn't a slut. She just wanted to make money for her kids, but then she got into the product deep, 'cause by that time Sanders was making it himself in a new lab at the hotel. He also owns charter boats and a mechanic's shop, and he orders chemicals up on the barge. Captains bring some of the really suspicious chemicals up

on their boats for him. So his shit is good. Clean and
strong. He calls it 'bulletproof.'"

"Nice, but hurry it up. I've got to decide if I'm going
to shoot you or not."

She smiled as if I were flirting with her. "You aren't
going to shoot me." And then in the next instant, she
gives me a hard stare, a stare that would make you
think she were bulletproof. "So, anyway this Bean girl
gets in way too deep. No money from dealing. No
money from the little lap-sitting at the card games.
She is getting paid in bulletproof dope, and eventually
heroin, which Wynn is also starting to get into."

"So, she ODs?" I offer, getting more and more worried about the time.

"No, she cuts a guy at the game. A big player,
and he slugs her so hard she falls and breaks her
eye socket, both of them actually, one side of her
face from the blow, and another . . . boom . . . from
the fall. She is messed up and she threatens to go
to the cops. She says she is done and she wants to
get clean. Sanders and my fucking boyfriend then
pump her full of so much meth that it fries her
heart and she dies."

"So, what about the Permanent Fund checks. I
heard she cashed them all, hers and her kids'."

"They took her post office key and got the checks."

"And you cashed them?"

"That's how they had the bite on me. I cashed the
checks. I say anything and it wouldn't take much to
track that down. I just wore a hat and sunglasses. Shit,

anybody will cash a Permanent Fund check. But it's definitely my handwriting on those checks."

"Where is her body?"

"That's the other thing about these douchebags," she whispered, as if we were just gossiping across the fence. "The plan was to dump her at her house and let the cops find her pumped full of meth and figure it was just an overdose. But . . ." Here she paused and her eyes began to tear up, and she stared off to her left at the painted concrete wall.

"But . . . ?"

"My dumbass boyfriend has sex with her."

"What? Come on, before or after he kills her?"

"Oh . . . you know him! He says she was all hot to trot for him, but I don't believe a word that sack of shit has to say. Like she was going to have sex with him after she cut a guy who wanted a blowjob."

"Wait . . . a blowjob?"

"The card player, she cut him bad. I told you. Now she has the player's blood on her and her clothes. Like, I'm sure she's feeling romantic. Fuck that guy."

"Love's a bitch, Sherrie." I pull the gun out of my pocket and point it at her. "Where is Blossom?" I asked her. "I have to find her, or kill you."

"So anyway . . ." she went on totally ignoring my gun, "they don't want to risk having the cops find any DNA. Of all the chemicals they've got stored, they don't have twenty gallons of hydrogen peroxide, which is what you really need to clean up blood."

"What? You learn that in biology class?" I asked her.

BABY'S FIRST FELONY   133

"Don't you watch any TV?" she shot back. "So, anyway they cut her up in the lab, then take her down to the fish plant in bags and one of the guys slips the parts into the waste grinder, and she's pumped out into the channel along with the waste fish."

"Wow . . ." I said, and I looked at her for several moments. A beautiful, hard, woman. "You need a new boyfriend, Sherrie."

"I do . . . have a shitty boyfriend, and yes . . . love is a bitch . . . and yes, I can help you find your daughter."

"Good, but first I need something."

"You remember that I'm your client. You are supposed to be working for me," she said rather petulantly.

I waggled the revolver in my hand. "Sherrie . . ."

"Okay. What?"

"Use that phone and call David. Tell him you want a bail hearing, right away."

"I will never make bail. No way."

"No, you won't. But you have the right to a hearing within twenty-four hours from your first request, and you have the right to be at that hearing in person. Once you make that call they have to hold your transport. They will keep you in Sitka until the hearing is over."

"They are planning to ship me?"

"Yes. They heard someone wanted to kill you."

"Oh," was all she said, and she reached for the phone and made the call, and as the PD phone was ringing she covered the mouthpiece and whispered again, "The guy who wanted to kill me . . . that was you, so it's okay right?'

"Yeah . . . as long as I find Blossom."

Sherrie held her index finger up to have me stand by, then she spoke in a sweet singsong voice to Rhonda, insisting she wanted a bail hearing. "Right. Now."

My stomach hurt, and the chemicals in my system seemed to unclench in my guts and in my head. I felt woozy, as if I had just clipped the red wire on a time bomb. I wasn't safe, but the clock had stopped ticking for the time being.

Sherrie looked at me and for the first time during the encounter she appeared more sad than I had expected. Sad enough to make me worry. "He would stash Blossom in one of two places. She has to be safe and she has to be hidden from everyone but my boy-friend." She said the word "boyfriend" as if she were spitting out a rotten piece of fruit. "Check his lab or the top-floor studio at the apartment house. The building has one small window on the back with bars on it and a padlock on the outside. The front door is reinforced, but the walls in the entire building are weak as a kitten."

She looked odd saying the word "kitten." Like a little girl made of clay.

"That's where she has to be."

Now, Your Honors, it was then that I asked her a stu-pid question, for despite myself I started to cry sloppy drunkard's tears. "Would he really kill her?"

And despite the years of torment, the sexual assaults, the beatings, and the thousands of things she didn't want to remember, Sherrie looked at me with something like sorrow. She said nothing, but her dark eyes lowered to the floor, and I sobbed as I un-cocked the gun.

Your Honors, I know that you read the transcript of Sherrie's police interview in which she said that I threatened her, and she was forced to help me commit these charged offenses, but may I assert that these were post-facto statements to the police, whom she did not trust at all, and she made them with one purpose only: to get as far away from these events as possible.

I stood up and wiped my tears with the back of my gun hand. I took some breaths and stuck the gun in the small of my back. The camera would not catch me as long as I hugged the wall.

"All right," I said, and I left the jail. Betty watched me go down the hallway and said something about my mattress that I did not understand.

The rain had an unsettling narcotic effect on me as I stepped from the doorway. I stood in the middle of the street and let the warm drops fall on my eyelids. My brain was burning, as if my skull had grown infinitely large and smoke was venting up and out. My thoughts felt scarred and tired.

I didn't have a plan as I stumbled down the sidewalk. Sanders had said to keep her on the island. As long as she was here she was within reach. This would have to do because I was not ready to shoot my former client with the dark hair and the crooked jaw, right in the middle of the jail and spend the rest of my life in prison. I would have to bet that he wanted her dead bad enough that he would keep the hold over me going to know that I was planning on killing Sherrie Gault soon enough.

The release of getting more time unleashed some strange pocket of confusion and drunken brio. My hands shook, and I was worried that I would call attention to myself if I bent down and vomited on the curb. Suddenly I wanted to take a nap, or perhaps I was already dreaming.

I know it seems that I had formed an intent because the record reflects, and Javier Diaz confirms in his statement, that I came into the Pioneer's Home maintenance shop and took a large sledge hammer and a steel bar. I might add, Your Honors, that I know Mr. Diaz from work, and I know him to be a very reliable person. But I honestly have no recollection of picking up the bar or the sledge, and since taking these items seems to be the least of my legal problems, I don't think you can call it much of a self-serving selective memory loss.

There is a large section of *Baby's First Felony* dedicated to the subject of stupidity, specifically about when to invoke your intelligence as a defense to a botched crime. More specifically it reads: *Never, under any circumstances, ask (or in any way imply to) a judge who is rendering a decision in your case, "Just how dumb do you think I am?" You will not be happy with either the answer or the result.* So, I realize that I go forward with my story at my own risk.

But let me explain just for a moment here, Your

Honors. There may be, in this world, some successful lifelong criminals. I have known only two. One was white and the other black. Both were involved in the marijuana and psilocybin trade well before the current legalization scare. These were quiet people of boring demeanor. They did nothing to draw attention to themselves; they drove the speed limit and were unfailingly polite to police officers. They did nothing florid or gaudy in their professional or private life. Both were happily married to women of plain appearance with even temperaments, they drove their ordinary Japanese compact cars to church every week and volunteered at their kids' schools. Neither of them used their own product and both sold only to a handful of customers whom they had known since childhood. They wore brown pants and old sneakers and rarely said "fuck." That is to say they led boring lives right up until the day they quit the game and moved to their villas in warm climates, which they had built with cash payments to local Christian contractors. Then the wives had cosmetic surgery and drove their Mercedes however fucking fast they wanted.

But every other criminal I have met is stupid. Stupid in that, like a reverse Rumpelstiltskin they had a knack for spinning gold into straw. This cannot be explained by mere bad luck or even racial or class inequality. (Remember I'm talking about the true criminal here, who is a small subset of the prison population. Most of the people in prison are addicts, mentally ill or low-level scofflaws and repeat offenders who simply have a hard time remembering the ever-increasing number of sanctions that they have to live under.) The normal stupid criminal is the person of limited impulse control who believes in their own gifts: the sucker who believes they can beat the odds. The young man who clings to his ill-informed impulses like the old woman with the golf glove who spends the last years of her life pulling on the slot machine handle over and over again, believing as they do, that their life of loss and disappointment is certain evidence that the Big Win is coming their way. This, in my opinion, describes most criminals including sometimes . . . myself.

But the odds don't accrue. Each pull remains the same, and your misfortunes are only a sign that you are doing something wrong. This is a long-winded way of saying, Your Honors, that as I drunkenly walked toward the hotel building with a large-caliber Bulldog stuffed in the small of my back, I may have been trusting the shitty decisions I've made in my life, and navigating by a drunkard's luck, but I didn't have a specific intent to commit a crime. I just wanted to find my daughter and bring her safely back home to her mother.

Apparently, I walked through the lobby and to the stairwell. I must have taken the iron bar and pounded out the locks to the lower stairwell and the laboratory door. I don't remember it, but I can't understand why anyone else would do such a thing. It was then that the scene began to focus in my memory.

The door to the lab swung loosely on its hinges.

There were no sounds clattering off the concrete floor or ceilings. I heard water running in a sink and the scratchy wheedle of a small radio. I poked my head around the corner and saw only one overhead fixture hanging in a shaded cage above some stainless canisters. I walked in and tried to stay low, but my knees were weak. I came to a metal table and again raised my head. In the alcove, where I had last seen the lieutenant's body wrapped in a tarp, stood the Sweeper standing over an open bucket. He was stuffing white substance into a glass pipe while rocking unsteadily on the balls of his feet. He did not hear my shoes scuffing the concrete as he tunelessly hummed to the music from the portable radio.

I remember standing up, pointing the Bulldog at him, steady on him now, a straight line from the barrel to the center of mass. I remember starting to tell him to get my girl. Then I remember the concussion and searing pain as he shot me.

Cordite, and the iodine taste of blood in my mouth, burbling out my nose. Pain that blossomed through my body and up out of my eyes, causing the world to go red and sparkly blue. Blood from my mouth onto the concrete. Footsteps and breaking glassware. The feeling that I was drowning in blood. Vomiting while face down.

Then I remember a voice as Robert Boomer knelt over me.

"Dude, what the fuck?" he said slowly and sympathetically.

"Sweeper . . . where?" I might have said.

"He booked it. I heard you were drunk-ass stumbling down the street, so I followed you from the center of town to here. What the hell, man, what about the plan?"

"No plan . . ." I said "Blossom?"

"That's why I followed you. She's upstairs at the Hillside. Your guy, what's his name, has a line on her. But he is fucked up, dude. They just bounced him out of McDonald's for trespassing or something. He told me about it. Shit, he may be telling everyone, he's drunk." He paused and looked me over. He opened my shirt and my jacket and turned me on my side that hurt like it had been struck by a branding iron.

"Dude, you been shot. That's messed up." I didn't know what to say to that. He took off his own shirt and started to apply pressure to the wound in my chest, but I pointed to the clean hotel towels in stacks on the corner of one of the lab tables.

"Clean . . ." I think I said waving my hands.

Then he looked at his own shirt in his hands, soaked in grease and chips of metal. "Yeah . . . yeah . . . better," he said and grabbed the pile and put pressure on the wound. Despite the pain, being on my side made it easier to breathe.

"It went straight through. Hit the lung, but I think it missed everything else. Lucky son of a bitch, Cecil."

I may or may not have felt lucky, as the world whirled then dazzled into an ice-shattered blue . . . to black, and I was gone.

Through the warm narcotic haze, which felt like eating apple pie in a warm tub of scented water, I heard a familiar voice, I was happy to hear the voice at first until I realized that each word pulled me up out of the bath and back into the world of pain.

"Cecil . . . a private investigator walks into a library and says in a loud voice, 'I'D LIKE A CHEESE BURGER AND SOME FRIES, PLEASE.'"

"Not so loud, Todd," I was able to croak out underneath my oxygen mask.

Todd in his dutiful way went right on. "Then the librarian says to the investigator, 'Sir, this is a library!' and the PI whispers very softly, 'I'm sorry, I'd like a cheeseburger and some fries, please.'"

"Where am I?" I asked my oldest friend and ward.

"You are in Sitka Community Hospital."

"How long?"

"Just twenty-four hours . . . they were going to fly you out, but the police wanted to keep you here."

"The police?"

"They are outside."

"Did they find Blossom?"

"Blossom is still gone. Jane is talking to them right now."

"I need to get out of here."

"No. Jane says no."

A door swung open behind Todd's shoulder. A patrol officer in a black uniform and thirty-five pounds of guns, cuffs, flashlights, tazers and radios, came lumbering in.

"Cecil, because you have been shot we need to ask you about how this happened."

"Lawyer." I said. Even in the drug-addled confusion of pain, I felt proud that I was able to follow the cardinal rule of *Baby's First Felony*.

He reached to his radio and turned down the volume. I saw his micro recorder with the red recording light lit. He leaned over my bed and gripped the rail.

"That must hurt like the Dickens, huh?" he almost whispered.

"Lawyer," I croaked.

"Why in the heck would you want someone who shot you through the lung, someone who almost killed you, why would you want them to get away?"

Your Honors, I wanted to talk with him then. There is some, almost physical, force that makes anyone want to explain themselves to a policeman. The worst part of it is the more confused and frightened you are, the more the impulse to talk works its way up and out of your mouth. I wanted to tell him about Sweeper and the Mexican drug mule who had been killed in the room. I wanted to tell him about Sherrie, the lieutenant, and the dead girl gone missing. I wanted them to arrest Sweeper for killing Thistle. But mostly I wanted him to use all his tools and his big, blunt instruments of the law to find our daughter.

I cleared my throat as best I could. Todd leaned in and let me drink a sip of ice water from a straw. I cleared my throat and spoke the magic words:

"I want to speak to my attorney."

He looked at me and frowned. The words were immortalized on his little tape recorder. Todd had also witnessed it. I could tell the cop wanted to spit on me.

"You can be that way, I hope it doesn't cost your little girl her life," was all he said. He hesitated a moment waiting for me to change my mind. When I didn't he turned and walked out the door.

I turned to the morphine drip and fiddled with the hose. "Is there a trigger or a button on this thing?" Todd pointed to the monitor box, "Button there," Todd said, and I punched it three times.

"It only works once," he said in his flat, irritating tone.

My eyelids started to grow heavy, and the warm tongue of morphine started licking my wounds, covering me with its kiss. Baked cookies and ice cream, my tenth birthday in my mother's arms. Morphine. How pleasant.

Until it's not.

The door opened a crack and Jane Marie stuck her head in. She was not smiling. "You didn't let him push that button?" She looked at Todd.

"He pushed it without asking. It was fast."

"Leave him . . ." I slurred now, I took off my oxygen mask. "Not Todd's fault."

"I know that," she said. "I know it's not Todd's fault." She would not look at me in the eyes.

"Cecil, I want to talk with you about your injuries, and"—here she looked over my head—"about your drinking. But I have to ask you two things."

"Go . . ." I said.

Her dark eyes bore into mine now, and the pain pushed up through the narcotic warmth. "Do you know where Blossom is?"

I opened my mouth but she interrupted. "And . . . why in the heck didn't you want to talk with the police?"

"I didn't talk to them now because I need a lawyer," I said.

"The policeman said you are under investigation."

"I don't doubt it," I said. Todd was shifting back and forth from foot to foot. Soon he would begin rocking back and forth, forward and backward, which was how his body reacted to what we think of as anxiety. He called it feeling itchy. It is painful to witness.

"The policeman said he wanted to talk with you about a body they found."

My eyelids started closing as if by their own will. Lead eyelids.

"Which body?" I asked, honestly not being able to keep track. Pain drugs don't cure pain, I was discovering, they smother it and you too, eventually.

"They said it was a man who used to be a client of the public defender. He was found just a few minutes ago, at the cold storage. He had been shot in the head."

"Weird," I managed.

"Why weird, Cecil?"

"Can't say . . ."

"Where is our daughter?"

I managed to look at her. Her eyes were red as if all the tears were gone and only pain was left.

"Give me a second . . ." I said. "I can find her. We will bring her back. But . . ."

"But what, honey . . ." she leaned in.

I looked at Todd, "But first I want to hear a joke."

Todd stopped his rocking and grabbed the rail. "I know one."

"I bet you do."

"Cecil!" she pleaded with me but Todd went on.

"What's the difference between jelly and jam?"

"Cecil . . . for God's sake." Jane Marie turned away and started for the door.

From the darkness I said, "I dunno . . ."

"Because you can't jelly a dick up your ass."

"Terrible . . ." I said. "Just terrible." Then a dark hand put its palm over my eyes, and I was gone.

I don't remember waking up, but I must have. I must have had a conversation with someone because when I woke up there were people sitting in my room as if we were having a meeting of lost souls. Todd was asleep in a chair next to my bed, and Gudger was curled up on the floor by the bathroom. He had his head resting on his fetid coat. The room was filled with evening darkness. Wind from a storm whistled through the air vents, and the lights across the street shimmered like needles against the black window-pane.

Robert Boomer walked in the room with a large floating balloon on a ribbon. The balloon had the words IT'S A BOY! written in blue lettering. I looked at him as if he were a unicorn walking into the moonlight. He walked over and tried to give Gudger a high five. When he didn't respond, Boomer leaned over my bed.

"Dude . . ." he whispered. I pointed to the balloon. "Yeah . . . sorry it was all they had."

"It's good." I said.

"Your man here told me that you needed to talk with me." For some reason he kept whispering.

"I don't remember," I said. "Cops talk with you?"

"The chief himself tried. He was pissed when I asked to speak to a lawyer." He was smiling now, bathing in the good memory of it. "Bastard," he said.

"What else do you know?"

Gudger began to stir, trying to stand. His breath smelled like acetone and his clothes were still soaked through. He sat on the foot of my bed.

"Yeah . . . I did like you told me," was all Gudger said.

"Blossom?"

"She's got to be in the top room, north side back by the stream."

"How do you know, Gudge?"

"They wouldn't let me in there. I got into every other room."

I looked at Boomer. "You still have what we need to get in there?"

"Yes . . . but Cecil. We can't just blow a door down and go in guns blazing. Shit. First thing"—his whispering words were running away with him—"if she is in there she's likely to get hurt, and second . . ." He looked around in the dark as if to check if there was anyone outside of our felonious circle standing near. "The second thing is you suck at it."

He stopped and looked at me, then stupidly handed me the balloon.

"I mean, look at you. You are shit with guns."

"Any idea what happened to Sweeper?" I asked.

"Well you didn't shoot him. Because . . . you know . . ."

"I know, I suck."

"I was going to say because I only heard one shot from the stairwell. Then the Sweeper barreled past me headed up as I was running down."

"And now he's dead?"

"Yep. No loss there. Some Mexicans found him in the cold storage, and they did the right thing and called 911. Head shot, but not a lot of blood where they say they found him."

There was a light tapping at the door. Gudger stood up and straightened his hair as if that would make any difference at all. He had left a muddy stain on the floor and now a brown stain on my covers. Before I could say anything, Jane Marie walked in the room with a package under her arm. Something wrapped in newspaper.

She was ashen, her face was twitchy, and she flopped the packet on my lap.

"I found this on our doorstep," she said. Her voice was soft and hoarse. A ghost voice. "I . . . I couldn't open it. It feels awful." Now tears were coming, and she put her hand on Gudger's shoulder to stay upright.

I looked at the wrapping, today's *Sitka Sentinel.*

There was a bright smear of blood in the creases where someone had folded the paper over whatever was inside. I pulled back a sodden fold.

Sitting there on my lap was a human foot, severed just above the ankle. The delicate foot of a girl with a toe ring on the longest toe.

I leaned over the side of my bed and vomited. Gudger stepped back and stared. "Whoa."

"Jesus fucking Christ," Robert Boomer said. He had backed away from the bed and was now peeking out of the bathroom.

"Does this mean she is dead?" Jane Marie was numb, staring at the foot as if it were a tarantula crawling toward her. "Cecil . . . that's her ring," she said, slumping slowly down on the bed as far away as she could get from the foot. Gudger held her shoulders. Robert Boomer came out of the bathroom and brought a towel to clean up the vomit.

"On her toe. That is her ring," she whispered, "Blossom's."

"She's not dead. She can't be dead." I was muttering now as if to myself. "Why would he let me know he had killed her if he still wanted me to kill Sherrie?"

"Cecil . . ." Jane said sitting on the edge of my bed. Her hands were shaking.

"She's not dead, Janie. She can't be. But we must find her."

Todd was staring intently at the foot. Perhaps he was the only one who looked at it in detail and with dispassion. He was studying it.

From this point on, Your Honors, I was in the country of painful rage, everything I say here cannot be said to be true, because at that point my mind was not in alignment with accurate recollection but only with finding our girl.

I pulled the IV needle from my arm. I sat up in the bed. My head became a cloud of steam, and I lay back down. The foot rolled off my leg, fully exposed now: the white stub of bone, the weepy red meat. Todd stood above my bed looking at it intently. He opened his mouth to say something but . . .

"Help me up," I said and broke his reverie.

He leaned down to pull me up. "I will come with you."

"No," I said, "just get me moving. I will be okay."

"No, I don't think you will be okay."

"You might get hurt."

"You are already hurt."

"True . . . but . . . just stay at home by the phone."

"No. I don't think so." If you didn't know Todd, you would have found his tone of voice odd for the circumstances. He is not argumentative, and I doubt he was actually worried about me; he was passively unemotional. He had simply made up his mind.

"Okay, we will figure it out on the way. But . . . there may come a time where you have to do something I say. You have to promise that the next time I tell you to do something, we won't waste time arguing about it. Will you promise me?"

"But what if you say . . ." he started.

"If I say to duck, you have to duck." I interrupted.

"If I say run to the hospital, you run to the hospital. You have to promise."

He thought a moment, and I could tell he was thinking of all the possible orders I might give, and he wanted, badly, to have me clarify every single one.

"Listen, Todd, we don't have time. Do you promise?" Getting him to say it was important. To Todd his promise is more than a sacred oath; it is the redefinition of the future.

"Yes," he said finally, but he added, "Do you promise not to drink alcohol anymore?"

I looked at the group in the hospital room. Gudger and Robert Boomer were probably the worst intervention participants, ever. Gudger was looking at me solemnly and he was shaking his head. Boomer just smiled, shrugged and was about to say something when I cut him off.

"Yes," I said. "I promise."

Jane Marie, knowing well enough not to put any faith in me, wrapped her arms around Todd's neck and hugged him. I started out the door when Boomer called after me, "What about . . . you know . . . the foot?" He pointed to the chunk of meat on the bed.

"I don't know," I said. "Bring it along with."

We pulled all the machines power plugs from the walls so their alarms went silent. I walked out first wearing Boomer's coat, and no one looked up. The rest walked out a few moments later after closing my door softly. Before joining us, Jane Marie started talking to one of her old friends who was the charge nurse for the night. The plan was to tell her I was sound asleep for the night and to try and let me sleep.

Rain fell through the pools of light from the streetlamps, and the wind was making frolicking black horses on the horizon as we walked through the storm.

The community hospital is about three blocks from the apartment house, we walked in a double line side by side. Boomer was lagging far behind, but as we got closer he ran to the front and came up beside me. He handed me the gun I had started off the day with, and I put it in my pocket. Gudger then caught up and led us all up along the slope of a hill. We cut through a well-kept suburban-looking street with nice lawns. The lights behind the curtains of the houses flickered with blue TV-screen light. We were a ragged line of ducklings following the homeless inebriate. Finally, by cutting between two houses we came to a bluff facing the ocean. Below us was the roof of the Hillside. Scaffolding and tarps had collapsed and a blue bulb holding about as much water as a residential swimming pool was now on the flat roof. As more rain fell, the edge of the tarp on the mountain side sluiced the excess water down the side of the four-story building. Raindrops fell in the pool, millions of circles intercutting circles.

Gudger walked back under the canopy of trees, and there on a tiny ledge was another campsite he had built from sections of blue tarp he had stolen from work. There was a fire with more former clients drinking from cups and bottles in sacks. Here were the lighted balloons of more hobo tents and tarps.

"I thought this would be good, you know, for getting to work, if I just stayed here," Gudger said.

The tired faces of six old men I had once represented stared up at me like flowers. Two I had gone to trial with; the other four had taken deals. They were wet and quiet, but they were there to help me. There because Gudger and Robert Boomer had asked them to come.

There was quite a bit of room under the tarp and Gudger had a tent in the far corner. He had a bucket gathering drinking water off one quarter of the tarp and the bucket was overflowing down off the corner of the ledge. Gudger went about building up the fire from construction wood, most likely taken from the scaffolding project. He heaped on splintered two by fours and one small oak pallet, while Boomer went to splitting other boards with a small hatchet. The fire pit was below the brow of the ledge so the fire could not be seen from the road or the apartment building.

I flopped on the moss stump by the fire pit. An old man on the sex offender registry offered me a drink, and I thanked him but declined. My lung was on fire, and it felt as if someone was tearing open the sutured wound. I wanted to throw up again, but as I settled into the damp moss I relaxed, and as the smoke snaked up and gathered under the tarp and I listened to the crackling fire, my stomach began to un-seize.

Jane Marie would not look at me as we sat around

the fire. She sat next to Todd and had her arms around him. She stared into the flames and put her head on his shoulder. She told him she was sorry. She was sorry and wished that he would go home, but Todd just looked down into the fire and shook his head.

"No," he said, "I'm fine here."

It was there, in that wet brush camp, Your Honors, that we made the plan to extricate Blossom from the Hillside Apartments. Jane Marie kept advocating that we go to the police, but I had long ago rejected that possibility, not just because it would most likely result in my arrest, but because I didn't trust them. If cops were having sex with young girls at this poker game, and my daughter was one of these young girls, then it would be much more convenient for the police force if my daughter were unavailable to testify against them— even if they had to somehow explain her death. But I did not tell this to Jane Marie. At that time, she did not know anything about sex and the police. I had messed this situation up enough without adding uselessly to her heartsickness.

As an aside, Your Honors, I'd like to restate that I am not, in anyway, anti-law enforcement, as has been alleged in some of the State's filings. My allegations against some of the local police are not based on some kind of "long-standing personal animus" as they wrote. To be sure, I have some different views, and our system of litigation is intended to be adversarial, but regardless I am not a cop hater.

I know as well as anyone that we live in a time of

intractable divisions, made all the more complicated
by information systems that feed our personal opinions rather than challenge us with the truth. We would
rather look at our own images on our computers than
learn the hard truths about our lives. The more we
hide behind our screeching, self-aggrandized public
personalities, the more we need a rigorous objec-
tive investigation to resolve our serious conflicts. I'm
sorry, Your Honors, but this is just a fancy way of saying
that you don't get to put someone in jail based on an
opinion, for opinions, as Todd will tell you, "are like
assholes, everybody's got one and most of them stink."
I firmly believe that policemen are not bad people, but
Your Honors, exceptions have to be carved out for the
ones who have sex with thirteen-year-old girls.

Of course, my accusations against these cops are
only my stinky opinion at this point. They have not
been subjected to rigorous scrutiny or investigation.
Yet, as you well know, Your Honors, Alaska has the
highest rate of domestic assault and sexual abuse
per capita of any state in the union. But to be fair, I
believe we have a higher number of people in contact
with mandatory reporters, that is people who have
to make reports to the police because of their jobs:
health aids and teaching assistants, clinic workers and
cops. Dealing with sexual assault takes its toll and
sometimes that toll leads them to gambling or drugs,
or the kind of sex that haunts them in the first place.
This is a long-winded way of saying that if Blossom
talked to a jury about having sex with a policeman,

that policeman would be looking at a possible twenty-five to thirty years. This would be reason enough to lead some well-connected cop or dope dealer to want to kill her.

We talked around that fire for hours and came up with a plan. We needed supplies, so Jane Marie made a list in her Rite in the Rain notebook that she always carries. I needed tape for my chest where the track line of the bullet had broken some ribs. We needed carpentry tools and some items for Boomer's explosives, including caps, wires and a detonator. We needed a sharp, sturdy knife in a sheath; bolt cutters; a cold chisel and a sledge, in case Blossom was bound up or chained. Though if she was seriously injured which it appeared she was, she was probably not an escape risk. We needed something to use as a grappling hook, some life preservers and a mask and snorkel. All of the people around the campfire offered good ideas on how to get our supplies. No one was too drunk to pitch in. One old drunk who had been caught driving under the influence four times in six years, said simply, "I got a cold chisel, if I can find the fucker," and Gudger thanked him for the offer.

"What if she is dead?" Jane Marie said, looking through the fire into the darkness. "What if she died of blood loss or shock?"

I shook my head and spoke to her even though she wouldn't look at me. I was trying to think of something comforting, something smart that sounded like I wasn't trying to equivocate in the face of certain tragedy. Something hopeful like what EMTs say to dying people on the road as their car teeters from side to side on its roof.

"She's not dead," Todd said flatly. "I know it."

"He's right . . . She can't be dead, Janie," was all I could add.

Sometime late that night or early in the morning, Boomer, Jane Marie, Gudger and three of the other jailbirds took off to gather the materials we would need. Todd stayed with me to keep the fire going. He helped me into a sleeping bag, placing some newspapers underneath me because my wound had started seeping blood again. The wound in the front still had some tubes for draining infection, which we left in and Todd made sure they hung outside the bag. I was sweating now, and my hands felt numb. My mouth was dry and I started to shiver. I asked Todd to put my feet above my head to help with the shock. Todd raised my head and gave me rainwater from a metal cup of Gudger's that he filled from the bucket. The water had some spruce needles in it but I didn't care. One of the old birds offered to douse my wound with vodka, but I thanked him and declined.

I slept for some time. When I woke, Jane Marie stood over me, and Todd was sitting propped up against the stump watching me like a hunting dog.

"I have some peroxide, antibiotic cream, dressings and tape. Sit him up and wrap the tape tight," she said to Todd, and he got to his feet. "I have this too." She took two syringes out of her coat pocket; they were small caliber and the needles were covered with different colored caps. She got on her knees and took my arm out of the bag. "I'll give you a little now to help you rest and then a little more before we go into the apartments."

"What is . . ." was all I got out before she stuck me in the arm with a needle.

"This is an antibiotic." She grabbed my arm and dug around with the other needle for a vein. "And this one is for the pain."

I closed my eyes as slowly a warm wave of relief folded over me like a blanket. "Where did . . . ?" I asked her and she shushed me.

"We still have some friends among the nursing staff at the hospital. They weren't happy to see you leave without permission, but when I told them someone was trying to kill you, which seemed obvious from the gunshot wound to the chest"—here she looked at me with raised eyebrows—"they saw fit to give me some supplies for you."

She held me upright and gave Todd instructions first on getting my coat and shirt off, and then in changing my dressing and taping me up tight.

"Thank you . . ." I mumbled.

"You can save the thanks for later."

The storm whistled and hissed through the trees. Rocks tumbled down the little stream that was running high on its banks, and the flames of the little fire under the tarp flapped back and forth as the gusts blustered through. I slept for a few more hours; I know that only because there was milky light filtering through the trees by the time everyone was back at Gudger's hobo camp.

I went over the plan, several times. Jane Marie corrected and added emphasis. The first priority was to get Blossom out. The second was to incur no casualties in our group, and the third was that there would be no serious injuries to the residents. To be clear, Your Honors, we felt our actions were a necessity. Even though that finding was not made by the jury at trial, it is none the less true. Our daughter was going to die, and this was our only recourse. That our actions resulted in millions of dollars in damage (the exact figure of the damage is still in dispute), and the relocation of eighty-four persons, was not part of the plan or intention.

Neither were we reckless in our actions, in that we did not disregard a substantial risk. We planned everything very carefully. That we "essentially destroyed" the Hillside Apartments, was not as a result of our actions but by the flimsy nature of the structure itself, the details of which were unknown to us at the time.

Or at least that's my argument.

We wanted to wait until seven-thirty in the morning. This would ensure that most of the residents would be awake and getting ready for work or school, and if they were still sleeping, they would be able to be woken quickly and exit the building. The sun was clearing away a few of the clouds as morning came. There was a pause in the rain for about a half an hour. We were all gathered and drinking coffee that Gudger had made and eating some eggs wrapped in tortillas that Robert Boomer had prepared over the fire, which had burned down to coals during the night.

While Jane Marie, Todd and I were finishing eating, and after Robert and Gudger had gone down to begin their work on the roof, I heard someone crashing through the brush on the hillside above. It was someone not worried about stealth, someone clumsy and struggling through the wet brush. It didn't seem like an attack, but I still gripped the pistol in both hands and held it in front of me. Jane Marie put the palm of her hand out as if to stop me. I lifted the gun toward the sound as the figure stumbled and fell down the last pitch onto the muddy little flat. I stood up with the gun leveled at his head.

David Ryder rolled over and looked up at me. "Jesus Christ, Cecil, put that gun away. You are inept with weapons." David Ryder, my boss, the assistant public defender assigned to Sitka, Alaska, had stumbled into camp.

"You thinking of shooting my black ass?"

"No," I said, and I put the gun down.

"Don't you know that black lives matter?"

"Yes, boss," I said, in the most contrite way I could manage . . .

"Give me that thing, for the Lord's sake. You are going to hurt someone." He took the gun from my hand. He looked me in the eye and said, "I need to talk with you."

"What are you doing here?" I asked, and as I did I

noticed Jane Marie twisting her wedding ring on her finger in the way she did when she was most irritated with me.

David looked at her even more sternly than he had looked at me. "Jane, you didn't deliver my message?" he asked.

"We haven't exactly been talking," she mumbled.

"But you did tell him about the plan? Should we be expecting more people to drop by?" I asked her, trying to curb the sarcasm.

"Don't start," was all she said.

Todd smiled at David and offered him some boiled coffee, which he took.

"Thanks, Todd." Then he looked at me. "Come into my office." We walked to the far corner of the tent and he gave me the benefit of his advice.

As you have read in the previous briefing, the jury appeared to give great weight to David Ryder's testimony and while I still maintain that our conversation was protected by attorney-client communications, and he should not have been compelled to testify as to that conversation, I do not deny, Your Honors, that Mr. Ryder, in general terms, tried to talk me out of my plans.

"Are you out of your God damn mind?" were his exact words after I described the specifics.

"He's going to kill her, boss. If she isn't dying or dead already."

"Go to the police. Go to the court."

"I can't do that. Sanders had the lieutenant in his

pocket, then he killed him. Do you hear me? He killed a police lieutenant. And by the way, the other cops were skulking around Sweeper's apartment when I tried to carry Thistle out of there. I have to think there are others on the take. I have to think there are others even more motivated to stay alive by keeping me dead or in jail forever."

"Go to the troopers. You have friends there, old family connections."

He was referring to my friendship with the highly respected Alaska State Trooper, Detective George Doggy, who had passed away more than thirteen years ago.

"I can't do it."

"Do it."

"Sweeper is dead. Thistle is dead. The Mexican drug mule is dead . . . I was standing right there when the last two were killed."

"You are bad luck, Cecil. Go to the police."

"He killed a policeman . . . or caused it to happen. Either way he owns the local police."

David threw up his hands, turned as if he were walking away, then quickly turned back. "The chief called me and said you are under investigation for the Mexican drug mule killing and maybe the disappearance of the lieutenant and Sweeper. Somehow they know that you had the money, and they're thinking you might be involved in a contract killing. It's a goat rope, Cecil. I had to call my supervisor in Juneau. It's gone all the way up to the Anchorage office and back. You are suspended as of now, and they are already working on your termination file. Which is the least of your worries."

"I want you to look at this." I walked over to the edge of the tent flap. Robert Boomer had sealed the foot in a plastic bag. It was a food storage bag. I held it up by one corner between the tip of my thumb and index finger.

"Oh my God," he said and turned away to gag. He dropped his coffee cup in the mud.

"What can I do to help?" he asked me when he stood up straight.

Gudger and Boomer worked on the roof scaffolding and the sluice, and by seven o'clock they had extended the taped-together tarps across the entire roof and rigged a makeshift water trough from the creek above the building on the hillside into the jury-rigged tarp holding tank. My attorney was stationed at the mouth of the sluice and worked at keeping it clear and free of rocks as we made a small lake on the top of the Hillside Apartments.

By seven-thirty, Gudger was down from the roof. Jane Marie dried him off and handed him clean coveralls that she'd brought from home. She combed his hair and gave him aspirin, water and just a sip of nighttime cold medication to steady his nerves. She also handed him a clipboard filled with whale sighting forms, of which she has hundreds. The forms and clipboard were intended to make him look official, for the next step.

The six jail birds stationed themselves along the main roads from the police station to the apartment. Their only assignment was to lay down drunk in the roads when the time came. This might buy us a few extra minutes.

Robert Boomer had gone home and then out to his concrete storage area, where he kept his private reserves of explosives. He took half a brick of plastic explosives, some rubber gloves, a blasting cap, a hand detonator that created its own charge so he didn't have to rely on batteries and about ten yards of yellow and red wire from the shed and placed them carefully in two carpenter bags. He also had a small water bottle filled with kerosene and had cut newspaper and wet alder limbs into small chunks, leaves and all, and stuffed into a five-gallon paint bucket along with two quarts of old engine oil. He then pounded the lid down on one side.

By eight o'clock the scaffolding and the tarps on the roof were full to capacity. The rain had started again and wind rippled on the surface of the small lake that shimmered in the tarps, while the two by sixes bowed and swayed as the wind continued to buffet the ridiculously frail structure. Once the tarp was full, David unhooked the sluice from the stream, then wiped his hands and walked up the hill to the road and drove back to the office to establish his alibi.

Todd and I took the bolt cutters, the sledge and cold chisel to the fourth floor and climbed a ladder to the roof, where we stood along the outside edge. This area of the roof was planked with rotten wood and was extremely slick. Jane Marie stood out on the sidewalk below to relay messages to Gudger and Boomer inside the building. Once Todd waved at her, she signaled to Gudger that we were in place, the plan was in play and the giant boulder of our work would start to roll back down the hill.

That things did not go as planned is a given. But again, it was not our intention.

Gudger went to a supply closet on the lobby floor and placed the paint bucket there. He doused the kerosene onto the papers in the bucket and threw a lit match in. He left the paint can lid partly on and the closet door ajar. Then he waited five minutes, until a nice column of smoke began to rise out of the closet.

At this point Robert Boomer began to improvise. He stood off to the side of the locked secret room and pounded on the door with his foot. He yelled, "Sitka Police open up!"

This, Your Honors, was clearly not part of the plan, but he did it. The door opened toward the inside on a chain. Two eyes peered out and a voice said, "Jesus Christ, it's early, you guys." Then he stood before them with what was reported as a "maniacal grin," and when they saw Mr. Boomer in his wet and incredibly greasy coveralls they knew they were not being treated to a pleasant visit from the SPD.

Now, Mr. Boomer had planned to use a quarter brick of the explosives to blow the door. But once seeing it open he refigured his calculations, and, reasoning that the door opened inward and had a chain holding it, he quadrupled the amount of explosives we had discussed using, and as he so colorfully said in his statement to the police, he made this decision "just for shits and giggles."

As the smoke rose up through the stairwell, Gudger and Jane Marie started pounding on doors and rousting people out of their apartments. They moved quickly and urgently giving them as little time to get out as possible. They started from the top down, and soon Robert Boomer was packing his explosives around the lock and the door frame on the apartment where Gudger was telling us that Blossom was being held. He had it wired up in less than three minutes. Five minutes later, all the other residents' doors were open and almost everyone was either out on the street or on the first floor.

The plan was for me to open up a small hole on the roof and start letting water in through a tear in the holding tarps. This would get the people in Blossom's holding room to hurry out. Boomer would let them go and then enter without blowing up the door. If they did not come out immediately, I would open up a larger hole to flood the floors and Boomer would blow the door. Then I would drop through the ceiling and Boomer would come in and free Blossom.

We assumed we would be able to communicate by tapping on the roof, and listening so we could coordinate each of our movements. One tap from me was "Ready."

Two was "Wait." We would let the people holding Blossom come out when they first saw the flooding. Ideally, we would use very little of our water reserve and none of the explosives.

But as you know, Your Honors, that was not how things worked out. For when I made the first hard tap on the rotten roof decking, Mr. Boomer blew up the door, and a good portion of the adjacent wall. The concussion of the blast caused the already over-stressed roof structure to collapse.

Tarps tore, and soggy wood gave way. A giant wave of clear rain water cascaded down through a large section of missing roof. Walls gave way, and door frames splintered as the wave sluiced down through the building. From the roof the great mass of water appeared like the smooth current of a cold river just as it breaks over the lip of a falls. The first wave of damage knocked me off my feet, and water grabbed my legs. Todd grabbed my hands; he lay flat over the edge of the roof, holding on to me. The hammer and chisel were gone but one leg of the bolt cutters was through my belt. Todd tried as hard as he could but the current against my legs kept sucking me down.

"Okay, Todd. You have got to let me go," I said as calmly as I could manage. The pain in my shoulder and lung was immense and frankly I wanted him to let go just to make it stop hurting.

"No, Cecil," he said and his voice was pitched high and tight.

"It's okay, buddy. Remember you promised. I'm going to go get Blossom and bring her home. You can drop me."

"Cecil . . ." he said, "I've got to tell you something important."

"Can it wait?"

"No . . . I don't think so, you see, that wasn't her foot. I know her foot and that wasn't B's."

I smiled at him, and even though the entire building was beginning to sag and shred apart, I was filled with a dull kind of relief because somehow, I knew he was right. Blossom hadn't been mutilated. I could hear nails shrieking as the roof began to pull apart. For some reason I thought of poor Thistle, her sad smile and her stringy hair, but before I could say anything the entire roof collapsed and a second wave hit us both, and I pulled Todd with me as I fell through the ceiling.

We tumbled, as if in the white water of surf. Clothes and sections of flooring floated around my head. I held on to Todd's hands until we jolted against a large timber frame section. Todd pulled away from me in the darkness. For a moment I saw sparks but they disappeared immediately. I grabbed on to a timber until the water level began to lower. Later, Jane Marie told me that water burst through the windows. She saw television sets exploding out of the white-water foam; she saw packages of diapers, beer bottles, poker chips like polka dots flying through the air then falling back into the torrent. She saw torn posters and needlepoint samplers still in their frames gushing out onto the streets. There were playing cards and dollar bills, packages of cheese puffs, soaked strips of insulation, soggy cigarette cartons spilling their precious packs and bits of wood with porcupine needles of nails sticking through them. There were dolls and plastic trikes, Tupperware containers, sacks of garbage and shards of glass flowing into the street like fish from a broken tank.

I held on to the post and the water lowered to my waist. I heard screaming. Boomer had a man by the legs who was floundering in the water. Todd hugged another support post. His glasses were crooked, and he was spitting out water from his mouth and coughing. I waded through what had once been a door and on the far wall, cuffed to a pipe, was Blossom. She was pale, and her old-fashioned dress was soaked through. She was shivering but standing on two feet.

When I cut the chain of her cuff with the bolt cutters she stared at me; her eyes were dark and her face expressionless. Hair in fabulous colors hung down like tentacles in front of her eyes; her lips were moving but no words came.

I heard heavy boots coming up the stairs. Boomer had turned to meet the firemen as they came up onto our floor. Boomer was dazed and confused he said. He had no idea what had happened. One minute he was visiting a friend to give him a ride to work and the next thing, boom . . . all hell broke loose. He carried the man whom he had grabbed by the legs in his arms now. Boomer had only come up to the top floor to see if he could help. A fireman told him to take the man down to the aid station being set up outside.

I held on to Blossom's hand and turned to Todd. "Remember. If the police start asking questions. You tell them you want to talk with your lawyer. Say those words to me right now, Todd."

"I want to talk to my lawyer," he said as he shivered in the wreckage of the room.

Blossom reached over to Todd and touched his cheek with the tips of her fingers.

"Hello B," Todd said, "it's good to see you."

Blossom started to cry and she turned to curl up in my arms.

"Honey," I asked her, "where is Sanders?"

She shook her head and sobbed into the hollow of my ear. "Daddy . . ." she said.

I was about to ask her again when four officers rushed down the slippery hall with their guns drawn and told me to get down on my knees with my hands in the air.

I had had her in my arms for less than twenty seconds when they tore her from me, then put me in cuffs. Jane Marie came up close behind them and took her daughter in her arms. Even after the cops ordered her at gunpoint to let the girl go, Jane Marie would not. She had one arm tightly around Blossom's waist as she walked down the hall to the waiting EMTs. Todd walked dutifully two steps behind and kept whispering, "I want to talk to my lawyer, I want to talk to my lawyer."

Gudger and Boomer drifted into the crowd of soaked apartment dwellers. Blossom went to the hospital with a police escort. Jane Marie was kept out of her daughter's room until she hired a private attorney to come and assert her rights to be present at any interview Blossom had with the police. The attorney also hovered around her to make sure she did not make any statements she did not want to give. They took me to the jail and did not even try to talk with me until much later. The cuffs left me with red welts, and when I asked for medical attention for my gunshot wound, which had reopened, they gave me a towel and some aspirin.

The inmates hooted and greeted me as a conquering hero when I came in, so much so that we were all immediately locked down. I lay alone in a cell on the thin mat, and even though my chest ached and blood seeped onto the towel, I felt something close to that narcotic blush of relief that Blossom was alive and standing on two feet. I slept soundly and dreamed of riding with her and Jane Marie in a small red dory on a calm river where crickets chirped from the long grass along the banks.

I woke up to the rattle of keys and the creak of a door swinging open. A fireman came in and changed my dressing by yanking off the tape from my chest, hair and all. A detective from SPD stood over me, happy as heck to see me wince and call out as the tape came off. The fireman tried to explain it was less painful to do it fast, and I seem to remember the detective chuckling.

Once the fireman was done, he told the detective that I really should be in the hospital and that at the very least they needed to get a doc in to see me, and the detective nodded without taking his eyes off me.

"Mr. Younger doesn't want to see a doctor," the detective said. "It would probably violate his rights somehow. That right, Cecil? You want to see a doctor?"

"I am fully cooperative, officer. Whatever you see fit. I'm in no condition to make my own medical decisions right now."

"See that, Ed? He doesn't want a doctor."

The fireman got up and left quickly. "It's not up to him" was all he said as the door clicked shut.

"We're going to hold you for obstruction of justice, illegal use of explosives in the commission of a terrorist act, burglary for entering the building illegally to commit said crime, a bunch of counts of assault in the second degree for putting all those people in fear of death, plus a few more things we are still investigating."

"Like?"

"Like the disappearance of one Mexican who flew in on Alaska Airlines, and no one can seem to find, and the disappearance of a Sitka police lieutenant."

"Okay . . . but my daughter is all right?"

"Yes . . ." and here he scowled. "Yes, glad to say she did not get killed by your stupid stunt. What were you thinking anyway?"

"You going to read me Miranda, or are you just going to skip that part?"

"I'm just curious . . . shit . . . you must not love her at all to try to kill her like that."

"Lawyer."

"You must not love your daughter at all . . . or you are as retarded as that guy you took care of."

"Lawyer. I want to speak to my attorney."

"I mean if you wanted to kill Blossom there have got to be easier ways, Cecil. Why don't you tell me the truth, and this will be a whole lot simpler. Just tell me. I don't think you're a bad guy. The boys outside say that you are a psychopath. They want to charge you with attempted murder of your daughter, and I told them I don't think he meant to do that at all. I said, let me talk with him, right now, today, and we'll get this sorted out."

"That's sweet. Lawyer. I want to speak to my lawyer."

"It's a big mistake not to talk to me. You know it. We can stack on these charges, and you will never make bail, and even if you beat every charge, you will still spend a year in jail sorting them out. That going to be easy for you, Cecil? Staying in jail with all your clients and former clients? How do you think they are going to treat you? Why not take care of it tonight? Tell us who shot you. We'll cut you loose and put him in here where he belongs."

"Truly, I'm touched by your concern, and I do want to fully cooperate with you, Detective, but only after I've had a chance to talk with my attorney."

"It's your choice. You know as well as I do. Lawyers just gum everything up. They get paid and you do the time. Isn't that right?"

"Put an egg in your shoe and beat it," I said, then added, "please." Just to enhance my prison thug credentials.

Of course, the detective was using the Reid technique, which is the standard training protocol for interviews in law enforcement: give the detainee a false choice, either you are a sick criminal who should be flushed down the toilet, or you are a good guy who just got caught up in circumstances and made a bad choice. What you really need is understanding and maybe some treatment, and how else are you going to get that understanding and treatment unless you tell us about these horrible circumstances? Good guys talk with the police.

The false choice works surprisingly well, considering, too, that most detainees are frightened and unsophisticated and believe that Officer Friendly is going to be there by his side all the way to make sure they get justice. Couple that with lack of sleep and often drug or alcohol interference with judgment, and most defendants make stupid and ill-considered statements to the cops. Lies are as bad as the truth, and once you start talking you are done. In the situation I was in, Your Honors, I was squarely in the possibility-of-terrible-statements territory. I was in pain and distress, my memory was spotty at best, and let's not forget the need to justify my actions to authority. All of these factors would have caused me to babble some nonsensical version of the events without having a calm moment to consider what was actual truth and what was fear talking.

"The truth is the truth is the truth," one detective used to like to say, and while that may be so, if knowing the truth were easy, we wouldn't need bartenders, or judges, or probably half as many detectives. The other problem with the "truth is the truth" worldview is that most people don't live in the world of truth. Most of us live in the world of self-justification. The hardest lesson for a young public defender to learn is that your clients, even in the midst of doing something completely antisocial, violent or self-destructive, feel *justified,* and it's this justification that they desperately want to communicate to Officer Friendly.

I mention this, Your Honors, only because even though you understand the Fifth Amendment and my right to remain silent, you know everyone who invokes it sounds guilty as sin . . . of everything. And while I am guilty of some things, I'm innocent of others, and the truth is the truth is the truth, hardly helps in parsing this out.

So, the detective walked out vowing to ruin my life for not unburdening myself to him. I closed my eyes and tried to sleep, but sleep would not come. A kid in a cell two down from mine was weeping and muttering to himself, and the pain in my chest ricocheted around my entire body, like a steel ball banging around under my ribs. A woman on the other side was screaming and swearing at the jailer, but that was far away.

The jailer gets all the prisoners food from the hospital, about a mile away. Sometime that night, before the lights went out, the jailer came in with food from the hospital in Styrofoam clamshells. Slice of turkey and gravy with canned vegetables, a slice of bread, and a carton of milk. What should have been warm was cold and what should have been cold was warm. Not that I complained. I scooped it all into my mouth with a flimsy fork. The young jailer whispered to me that a doctor would come see me when he finished his clinic hours.

"Just hold on, Mr. Younger. I'll get him here for you." I must have looked bad because the jailer looked worried and spoke in a soft voice of real concern. I started to worry about my health for the first time. I really didn't want to mess up this guy's shift.

They locked us down again after the dinner boxes were picked up. By this time I was sweating and had the chills. My head felt as if it were splitting open and each breath felt like a knife blade. I could not sit up, and I couldn't roll over. Sometime after lockdown the hallway door swung open, and a new prisoner was brought in. He wore jail-issued green scrubs, several sizes too big, with brown plastic slippers on his clean white socks. He carried his bedding and a towel in his arms. They opened the door to the cell next to mine, then Wynn Sanders walked in and sat on his lower bunk. They locked the door as he turned to stare at me in my bunk.

"Mister Younger," he said.

The young jailer came to the front of my cell. "Cecil you have a lawyer visit. You want me to tell her to come back?"

I reached over and pulled myself up by the edge of the upper bunk. It felt as if I were pulling a tooth. "No, I'll see her," and I made it to my feet. The dressings on my chest showed blotches of red. They didn't give me a scrub shirt for fear of turning it into a medical waste problem. I held my left arm across my chest and used my right to hang on to the bars as I walked down the hall.

"Good luck, young man." Sanders said as I passed.

It was a very young woman who was waiting for me in the interview room. The young jailer very gently cuffed me to the bar and offered to get both of us a cup of coffee. We declined, and he closed the door softly.

"Hello, Cecil, I am Wendy Sasserman. I work in the appeals division of the Anchorage PD. I've been sent down to represent you." She had long brown hair that covered her shoulders. She wore a heavy sweater and had a wet raincoat over the back of her chair. She looked as if she were heading out on a fishing boat.

"How did you get here so quick?" I asked.

"They've been wanting me to come down here since you first dropped off the map."

"Are you going to represent me on these charges? Have you entered an appearance with the court?"

"Right now I am here to help you make good decisions. Of course, if you are charged with felonies you may want to get your own attorney, or you will have to go through the vetting process for a publicly funded attorney if you can't afford one. But right now, I am here to help you."

"Ah . . ." I said, trying not to sound ungrateful, but failing.

I had heard of her, Harvard Law, a savant of some sort: the girl wonder, eccentric with a big brain. They sent her down to get a read on just how badly I had screwed things up. But at this point, the agency's interests and mine were in alignment, so I could somewhat trust her.

"Do you have any great desire to tell me the whole story?"

She looked at me and pulled at a strand of her hair and fingered the end of it as if there might be a piece of gum stuck there.

"No. No great need."

"That's fine, we have time, but is there something that is going to change or disappear that we should discuss? Something I should be sure to preserve?"

"Just my own life, and maybe the life of Ms. Sherrie Gault."

"Ms. Gault is no longer a client of the public defender. We conflicted out of her case because of your . . . activities. We can't help her because you became involved, how should I put this? Extracurricularly . . . that might be it . . . in the investigation of her case."

"Is she here in the women's side right now?" I asked.

"Ms. Gault has been released. Her new attorney has worked something out for her. Neither David nor I know the terms as of yet. I just know she is out."

"Can you tell me what charges I'm looking at?"

She made a little girl's face, as if she were worried about being stung by a bee. "Jeepers, it's a long list they are discussing. I'm sure the detective tried to scare you with it." She looked directly into my eyes. "I understand you did not make any statement but lawyered up immediately, is that right?"

I nodded in the affirmative.

"Were you drunk, or high, under the influence of anything when they spoke to you?"

"I had some painkillers in my system but I was clear-headed enough by the time I got here."

"Good." She smiled, seemingly happy that the bee had flown off. "We'll get the tapes and make sure. Have you spoken to anyone else, on the phone or visitors?"

"No."

"Again, that's good." She picked up the same strand of her hair. "And I don't have to tell you that they will be listening to everything you say, in your cell, on the phone, in the visitor's box."

"Yes . . . I know."

"Right now they are holding you on a single count of assault one. One of the residents of the apartment house you destroyed suffered some injuries. They are also holding you on a burglary. But of course, they are talking about more. Are you sure there isn't going to be something that we need to nail down right away?"

"How is my daughter?"

She stopped and looked at the yellow pad on her

lap. She seemed sad again. "She is being treated in the hospital."

"What is Wynn Sanders doing here?"

"He was arrested on an assault and a kidnapping, and also a misconduct with a weapon."

"Is Blossom the complaining witness?"

"Yes . . ." Again her voice seemed softer now.

"Is the charge against Sanders a sexual assault?" Just saying the words caused tightness in my throat, and a foreign feeling of rage began to sizzle in my chest.

"I don't know . . ." she said. "The detectives wouldn't tell me much."

"Are they going to arrest anyone else associated with the . . . what should I call it? The flood in the Hillside Apartments."

"They have people of interest . . . those are the detective's exact words."

"I suppose that I have been fired from the agency . . ." I pulled against the cuffs that kept me in my chair.

"As of two days ago you are on paid leave. That's all I can tell you." Now she wouldn't look at me.

"You're not my lawyer, are you?"

She paused and stared at me for a moment. She had a fine poker face.

"I think the main office sent you down here to see how badly I've hurt the agency."

"I will help you, Cecil. First, say nothing to anyone about your case. Second, you must be careful in jail.

Your bail right now is three hundred thousand dollars. I imagine we can get it reduced, but I'm guessing you will be spending some time in jail until we can get an agreeable bail proposal arranged." She picked up her yellow notebook. She hadn't taken any notes. "What else?" she asked me.

"May I speak to you once a day?" I looked at her leather dress shoes, they were soaked through but not muddy. I'm thinking she visited the scene.

"We can try for that. What are you looking to discuss?"

"I want you to find out how my daughter is, where she is, and I want to know everything you can find out about the Wynn Sanders case."

"You understand that is not exactly my mandate. I'm here to represent you."

"Will you do it? Will you keep me up to date on my daughter?"

She looked at her shoes. "I can't pass information on to you that you may be able to use in the commission of a crime. Do you understand me?"

"I'm not going to commit a crime. I'm in jail."

She leaned in next to me. I could feel the heat from her cheek against my own. I could smell the weird hippy scent of her shampoo. "I would not blame you for . . . taking action against Mr. Sanders while in jail, and if you want to know the truth, I think that's what the cops want you to try, but if you assault or kill Sanders while in jail, and they learn that I abetted you in anyway . . . then . . . well then . . ."

"That would be very bad for your chance to get appointed to the bench during a Republican administration." She smiled at me as if I were a new puppy. "But will you do it? Will you give me updates every day?" She was silent. "You don't want to be a damn judge anyway . . . it's like grading papers. Not nearly as fun as this."

She raised her eyebrows. "Yes, one call a day. Let's say noon if you can manage it. I know it's difficult to schedule anything in jail, but if I don't hear from you for two days, I will call the jail and have you brought to a phone."

"You going to keep to this promise?" I said, and she stopped smiling immediately.

"I had a mentor when I first came to the agency. He was brilliant and a very good lawyer. He told me right off, 'Don't make your clients any promises. But if you do make them a promise . . . keep that promise if it's the last thing you do in life.' So, yes, Cecil, I promise. We will talk tomorrow. I will be in town poking around."

"Tomorrow then."

"Yes." She let out a long sigh that bubbled in her lips like a horse sneezing. "You are in a heap of trouble, Mr. Younger. Don't do anything to make it worse."

"I promise," I said, then I smiled at her.

As I walked down the concrete corridor between the cells, my former clients hooted and yelled. Some made kissing sounds and someone threw a napkin. One pedophile I knew quite well pantomimed ramming a dick in his mouth. When I stared at him and took a step toward him, he stopped and said, "Hello, Mr. Younger. It's nice to see you here." These might have been the old jailbirds up in the woods, but of different circumstance and temperament.

"Yeah . . . nice." I said, and then walked past his line of vision. When I lowered myself onto my bunk, my lungs were burning and sweat was dripping down my face.

"How you all feeling?" Wynn Sanders asked me from the front of his cage. I didn't answer, but I closed my eyes. Then his voice rang in my head as if in a fever dream, and I remember others talking and some booing. Mostly, I remember his voice pelting down on me like golf-ball sized hailstones.

"You think a Jewish lawyer is going to stop a piece of sharpened plastic from going between your ribs?"

All the sounds of the jail echoed around the concrete walls. The ubiquitous sound of the television clattered and smeared the sounds of the men grunting out their pushups or slapping playing cards on the hard floor. Some men ranted and some stifled their tears. But Wynn Sanders didn't relent.

"I'm tickled pink, I really am. Seeing you in here. A man of the people, a public servant right here with all your flock. Is all your talk about the rights and protections going to protect you here? This is the law of the jungle here, Mr. Younger. You got to sleep near all your drunk Indians and mongrels, the slaves and sons of slaves? Tell the truth now, son, you always felt you were better than them didn't you, now, Mr. Younger? How does it feel, son, to have your precious institutions abandon you, all your rights and protections on the other side of those bars? Are the government workers digging a tunnel to get you out? Well don't expect them anytime soon because they only work seven hours a day." He was almost whispering now, but still it burned. "You wrecked the innocent and aided the guilty, boy . . . and for all that you won't even get a retirement check."

He started speaking louder. Clearly wanting the others on the block to hear him now. His voice fell into the cadence of militant oratory. "We are in here together, Mr. Younger, prisoners of the Zionist Occupying Government, but I have a plan."

His voice rattled around the block in the blur of the background noise of men passing their wasted time. "You know why the government is so rich, Cecil? It feeds on the work of others like a dirty little bug. Even our president, who betrayed us so blatantly, is the descendant of money lenders. He and all his operatives make wealth out of nothing, and they educate their young to do the same. Oh, they're smart. It's foolish to think otherwise. They didn't get to where they are by being stupid. They invented usury; they invented homosexuality in the ancient world. Their forbearers in Greece invented homosexuality, and it spread like a cancer all over the world. You know why? The government only creates something out of the work of others. Like homosexual sex, it produces

nothing. They pay people not to work and create abor-
tion factories. That's the only thing this government
can produce."

"Wow," I said. "I don't think you are making friends."
A cackle rose up around the tank. Men started laughing and cheering as if they had been in on the joke.
The kid who had been crying was now starting to bang
his head against the side of his aluminum toilet bowl,
and he sent up a howl like a wounded dog.

"Check it out, boy. Look at this." One of the men
held his forearm out and around the corner, he had
two stylized 8s inked on his arm with strange lightning
bolts above and below. "I still have my culture and
heritage. What have you got? I hope you got some
lubricant . . ." And the howl rose up and echoed
around the tank as more men started banging against
their toilets.

I closed my eyes and prayed for sleep. The young
jailer came in and turned off the TV as punishment for
the disturbance. Then he turned off the lights. There
are no windows to the outside, no bars through to
the outside world. I had lost track of time. The howls
of complaint rose for a few minutes or weeks, until
it became clear that no one outside cared anymore.
There was nothing left to do but sleep, or pray, or
desperately masturbate in the bunks, which some of
them did.

Wynn Sanders wanted to dominate me now. Perhaps he wanted to goad me into a fight so that he
could kill me. I wasn't sure then, and I'm still not

certain now. Even after the horror that came later, the motivations of Sanders remain a mysterious rage.

Through the darkness, the sounds of the jail played around me. The television came back on, and in that fluttering blue light they served our meals in the flimsy foam cartons from the hospital. I only drank some lukewarm milk from a waxy box. I vaguely remembered the young jailer leaning over me and at one point taking my temperature. At some point another man came in and gave me shots then changed my dressing. I heard an argument out in the booking room through the iron door: two men yelling at each other.

"Wake up, Mr. Younger . . ." a voice from close in cut through the fog, "they say you're going to die in here."

I wanted to vomit but nothing came. Blue light flared, and voices rattled around my skull.

His voice nuzzled up against me in the dark. "I think their observation is quite prescient, don't you?" Even in my stupor I could recognize Wynn Sanders trying to impress me with his vocabulary. "In a way, I almost envy you. Soon enough you will be dead and in the kingdom of Satan with my dear little girl."

I tried to think of something to say as he paused. I could hear him grunting, pushing up tears from his gut. "My precious baby angel . . . whom you sent to hell." His voice was a hysterical combination of tears and laughter, a broken soul with no more worldly currency left to spend.

I did vomit the milk up finally. The jail became a

fever dream of lights and buzzing door alarms, men in uniforms moving around and inmates complaining. I remember being loaded onto a skiff and floating down a long hall. I remember red and white doors opening into a long, long hall, filled with cabinets, tanks and hoses. Someone sticking me in the arm again, and someone stripping tape off a roll. Then, a siren, and, Your Honors, I felt a vague concern, like a child in her bedroom, hearing the siren and worrying what tragedy she was rushing toward. Where in the dark night of rain and wind was the person that needed help, who needed these fast trucks and men in uniform? I was flying now and fine. All that was wrong with me was milky vomit on my prison uniform and, of course, the prison uniform itself . . . but apparently I was flying up and out of the jail.

I awoke to a beeping machine and the soft squeak of rubber soles around my bed. I had catheter tubing up my penis, and, apparently, my fever was dangerously high. I looked around and saw a woman sitting by my bed. She had a cell phone and a notebook on her lap. Her hair was long and unkempt.

"There he is," she said sweetly and leaned in over the rail of the bed. "I wouldn't worry, Cecil, if you die, we will have one hell of a lawsuit." I could not bring her image into focus. "Blossom will be able to go to any college she wants to attend." The voice appeared to be generated directly in my brain. The image of the woman spun, then dissolved, as I went back to sleep.

I woke to rain pattering on a shiny glass

windowpane, just beyond a bright pool of light. I had cold packs lying over my chest and one draped like a piece of warm meat over my forehead. I felt faintly euphoric, as if my brain had been lightly cooked, and then doused in ice water. Which I suppose it had. The nurse, seeing my eyes open again leaned over and said, "Mr. Younger, do you know where you are?"

"No," I said but then looking up into her angelic face I said, "But I'm awfully happy to be here, wherever that is," which is probably a pretty jailbirdy thing to say. I got that indication from her wan smile and her tone of voice when she said, "Well don't get used to it. We're going to get you better, and then you are going right back to jail. You can have some ice chips to suck on now if you like."

"Blossom," I said.

"No. My name is Jill," was all she said. I believe I asked to see my daughter three times, but I got no clear response, only that I was allowed no outside visitors. Then I answered her questions about my medical history without asking for a lawyer. I did this only because I hoped to soften her up about the visitor situation, and I wasn't quite sure that I hadn't already died, so her comments about going back to jail had a vague and sinister meaning.

"You're getting nothing more from me, sweetie," her angel mouth formed the words. "I'm in enough hot water if they find out I gave Jane those supplies." She kept smiling and starting asking me questions again.

Answering questions exhausted me and soon I was

back asleep. When I woke Wendy Sasserman was sitting by my bedside. Again, she had a yellow pad on her lap, and she was playing with her pen by twirling it over her thumb and around her fingers and flicking it back into her holding position with one quick snap. This is a recognizable nerd tic that shows the influence of good schools and hovering parents. At least that is what I have always believed.

"So, you are alive?" she said.

"So far." There was gray daylight and rain falling past the window now. "Did I dream that you were here earlier?"

"I keep my promises, Mr. Younger."

"You thought I might be worth more dead?"

"Stop . . ." She pulled a strand of her hair off her shoulder. She must have developed a boatload of personal tics at whatever Ivy League school she graduated from, Harvard, Princeton, I couldn't remember now. "I merely said that they had treated you horribly, and we would have sued the heck out of them if you had died in there."

"I'm sorry to disappoint." I started to unpack the old icepacks from under my bedding. The packs were body temperature now and felt like slugs snuggling against me for warmth.

"No disappointment, I hate civil actions anyway. Boring. You are always trying to reduce life into money. What's the figure? What's the amount?" She examined the ragged ends of her hair. "Soul crushing," she whispered as if I were not there.

"Blossom, what is the report?"

"Oh . . ." she said brightly and opened up the yellow pad perhaps ten pages in. She had the section tabbed. "Apparently, she was not sexually assaulted within twenty-four hours of the exam . . . which is obviously good."

"Obviously," I said. Truthfully, Your Honors, at this point I was not happy with my legal representation.

"But . . . she was clearly abducted and physically injured. Let me look . . ." and she read from her notes: "Contusions, abrasions on wrists and ankles, bruising on throat and petechiae in both eyes, indicative of a throttling injury . . ." She looked up at me as if she were reading my own dental report. "Two black eyes and defensive bruising on both forearms, possible chest injury, no broken ribs, but possible separation of rib structure in three places. Her rape kit showed no evidence of recent penetration, but her hymen was not intact. There was no redness, bruising or swelling in the genital area, toxicology swabs were negative for second-party secretions of any kind."

"How is she? How is her condition emotionally?" I was closing my eyes and leaned back on the pillow, grateful that my lawyer was so bloodless about this.

She flipped another several pages and read: "Tearful when brought in, but more proximate to this report she was calm, communicative and oriented in all spheres, with periodic bouts of silent noncommunication."

"Thank you," I said, and I meant it, "Did she say who hurt her?"

Ms. Sasserman closed the pad and looked up at the light. "Her mother would not let me speak with her. But the police arrested Mr. Sanders right after they interviewed your daughter. They have arrested no one else. Grand Jury is on Friday."

"Who do you think they are going to indict on Friday?"

"I know Sanders is on the list because your daughter is set to go over to the DAO on Friday."

"All right."

"And the DAs are going to indict you as well."

"What's your recommendation?"

Again she looked up at the ceiling as if she were looking for heavenly counsel. "I'm going to give you a choice. It's an honest and free choice. Do you know what I'm saying? I'm not sure what you should do at this point because I don't know the facts the way you do. But we have a chance to get you some consideration. I know a cop . . . a trooper."

"No," I said, perhaps too loud, perhaps too quickly.

"He is from the Major Crimes unit, stationed in Anchorage. I've worked with him before. He has no ties to your department here. He has also been involved with statewide internal affairs. He's been brought in on local corruption cases and police shootings. His opinion means a lot."

"To whom?" I asked.

"To the people who are deciding what your life is going to look like for the next ninety years."

I fell back asleep when she left. It was pitch-dark

outside with diamonds sparkling out the window when I heard voices outside my room. Another argument. I pushed the buzzer on the side of my bed, and as the nurse came in I saw a glimpse of Blossom's head. The nurse quickly closed the door. I heard pounding on the door and Blossom crying. I was out of bed and wheeling the IV pole across the floor before I even recognized the searing pain. I had reached the length of my catheter, and I stopped suddenly and spun around. My legs gave out as the nurse held me under my arm pits and swung me back to bed.

"Daddy . . ." I heard her say. "Daddy . . ." then the sounds of rubber heels on linoleum and the baritone whispers of large men taking her away.

"She can't come in here. She should know better," the nurse huffed as she tucked my sheet in. I pushed up against her palms holding me down on the bed. I said my daughter's name, three times over. The nurse fiddled with a tube on my IV, and warmth spread over my body and disappeared.

It must have been the next morning when I woke to the sound of wooden chairs being moved next to my bed. When I opened my eyes I saw David Ryder smiling by my feet. By my head was Wendy Sasserman, who must have been dressed for court, either that or she was planning to attend a funeral. Sitting directly at my bedside was an older white man in a sports jacket and no tie rigged through his button-down shirt. He had a chiseled jaw and graying hair. He had the features I imagine someone would want to carve into a mountainside someday. I could see by how his sports jacket laid that he was carrying a gun.

"We don't have a lot of time, Cecil. I'm sorry to wake you up. This is Trooper Brown. Ray Brown."

He smiled at me as if I were a prized hunting dog who had gotten mixed up with a porcupine. "How ya feeling?" he said.

"Don't say a single, solitary thing," David said, and I looked at him, my friend and the author of *Baby's First Felony.* "We need to get a few things worked out." Wendy grimaced and Trooper Brown sat smiling, occasionally rolling his eyes as my lawyer and my possible coconspirator worked out the terms under which I would talk with the cops.

Your Honors, I have spoken here about my attitude concerning the police. I consider myself open-minded, in that open-mindedness has helped keep me from being blindsided by circumstances with my clients. But I'd like to mention something here quickly about the general attitude among law enforcement concerning defense investigators: often the professional police detective sees the world in black-and-white terms. There are good guys and bad guys. Most cops feel that the defense investigator is not simply a bad guy but the parasitic worm that feeds off the corpus of the bad guy. They would be condescending toward me if they could just choke down their disgust.

I'm telling you this so that you will have an appreciation of my trepidation in talking with Trooper Brown. Once we were properly introduced and cleared to talk,

I sat with the cop and I told him the entire story, just as I related it to you. Why did I do it? I could tell you that I had been shot, and I was tired, my wife was angry and my daughter had been traumatized, I was honestly scared and uncertain about the future, I was out of ideas, and I felt sheepish about all the bad decisions I had made in my past, particularly the ones I had made in the last forty-eight hours. All those reasons were true, but the real truth was that deep in my reptilian brain I was no better than any of the mopes who had come before the bar and had been given a public defender. I did it because my lawyer told me to, and she must be right because she was free to go, and I was headed to jail. And . . . this is the hardest thing to admit, I was tired of playing the chess game of crime my life had become, and I thought the trooper would help me out. Like I said, Your Honors, I was no better than any other mope who ends up in cuffs.

But in the end I did have another motive. I told my lawyer I wanted something in return. I would spill. I would tell the trooper every last thing about the destruction of the Hillside Apartments, but I wanted immunity from prosecution for all my accomplices. Every possible one. I wrote names down: Jane Marie, David, Todd, Gudger and even Boomer the bomb maker. I would tell the story, but none of it could be used against them. Once he heard it he could not work on the prosecution of any of them.

She excused herself, and I watched her speak with the trooper through the tiny glass window in the door.

She spoke and showed him the piece of paper with the names. He frowned but nodded. Then she walked back in.

"All right," she said, "let's do this."

The detective took some notes and made copies for Ms. Sasserman. He was polite and well-spoken, nodding his head within the measured beats of our conversation, and was apparently sympathetic at the proper times. In short, I spilled my guts to him, which made David Ryder nervous at first, but eventually I wore down everyone's resistance. I have to say here, Your Honors, that the troopers and the district attorney's office were almost as good as their word about the immunity for my friends. They never came near Todd or my family, and my friend and former employer David Ryder was well-equipped to take care of himself. Gudger and Boomer had old probation conditions that the State of Alaska did not feel they could overlook, including the pending charges that they both already had over their heads. So their participation in the whole Hillside Apartment affair cost them, and they paid the price.

But at the time I told Trooper Brown the whole story to protect my friends. Then the trooper stood up and walked out the door. He did not shake my hand. Wendy Sasserman followed him out into the hall, leaving David and I alone looking at each other.

"Jesus . . ." David said finally.

Wendy walked in and slapped her pad against her leg. "You are going to jail, Cecil," was all she said.

Once I was able to stand and pee and start complaining about being in bed, they sent me back to the
Sitka jail. Wynn Sanders had been shipped to Lemon
Creek, the regional lockup in Juneau. I settled into a
rack in Sitka and waited. I could have approved addi-
tional visitors. Todd came to see me twice. Through
thick glass he spoke over a ratty phone connection
while he peered at me on the jail side of a tiny concrete closet. He said that B was not able to visit, and,
while Jane Marie was approved, she had told him that
"it wouldn't be helpful" if she came to see me. He said
that Jane Marie was fine, but he could hear her crying
sometimes at night. He said Blossom appeared okay to
him but she didn't like talking much.

He also told me this joke: "A polish man went to the
eye doctor . . ."

"Hold on, Todd, we talked about Polish jokes . . ."
I interrupted.

"I know but I don't think this one is disrespectful,
but I'm not sure. I don't think it makes fun of anyone's
lack of intelligence. But maybe you can help me." He
pushed his broken glasses up his nose and squinted at
me through the smudgy lenses. I could see the greasy
imprint of a delicate hand on his side of the glass.

"So . . . anyway. He goes to the eye doctor and
the doctor shows him some small letters that read:
CWVYZTIC. The doctor says, 'Mr. Wassilie, can you
read any of these letters?' and Mr. Wassilie says, 'Read
them? I know the guy!'"

He looked at me through bulletproof glass, with

purely honest confusion. "I don't get it, Cecil, but other people seem to laugh, and I don't know why."

I held my palm flat against the glass. "They laugh because it's funny. It's a play on how Polish names are spelled. It's not disrespectful. It's funny. You should keep telling it. Tell it to Blossom. She will like it."

"I will, Cecil," Todd said, smiling and obviously happy with himself. I left my hand on the window, and Todd awkwardly put his hand up on the other side.

"Tell Blossom the joke is from me if you remember." I wiped tears away with the back of my hand holding the receiver.

"I will, Cecil. I better go now."

And he did.

The days in jail flowed like a toxic river, one to the next. Television and watered-down coffee. Men complaining of different kinds of withdrawal: from cigarettes and methamphetamine, to heroin, women, iPhones, and porn. Men longed for the things they abused and things they had forgotten they had loved: a crisp apple, or sweet tea served with ice cubes, or steaks done medium rare that can be cut with a kitchen knife. Jail teaches you nothing so much as covetousness and the fixation on desire. And if you were of a Buddhist frame of mind this is the perfect petri dish for cultivating suffering. If you are denied all the sweetness of freedom, you either steal it wherever possible, or you devalue it, acting as if you never needed freedom in the first place.

Life went on with updates on Blossom's health and

the hope that Jane Marie would come to the glass cell for a visit. Todd came by from time to time, and he always said that Jane Marie was doing fine. He did not mention the crying, and when I asked about it he made a sour face indicating to me that he knew something but had been asked not to talk about it. For Todd, not talking about something he knew about was both difficult and uncomfortably close to lying, which he did not do. So I did not push him for any more details.

Once he came to the jail and held up a piece of paper with Jane Marie's handwriting, all it said was, *It is hard to love you, Cecil, but I do.* He watched me read the note, and he folded it back up and put it in his pocket. Then I told him to thank her for me, and he nodded that he would.

The days went on like this, until one evening three cops came in and told me to stand up. They fitted me with cuffs in front and ankle chains and took me to the airport. They pulled curbside and the cop sitting on my right turned to me and said, "There are two ways this can go. The way that is easy for you, where you cooperate and do everything you are told. Or the hard way in which we cuff you tight behind the back and basically carry you on and off the plane. One is very painful and the other is almost enjoyable. It's up to you."

"We are on an island in the North Pacific. Where am I going to run?" I asked, and when I looked at the two officers in the back with me I recognized them as the two who had come to Sweeper's apartment that first afternoon when I tried to carry Thistle out of the place.

"I remember you, Officer. You did such a great job protecting that girl," I said, knowing I shouldn't have.

"Mr. Younger, I have a conversation control device. Am I going to need it?"

"A conversation control device? Did you borrow it from your girlfriend?"

Your Honors, this would explain the horrible pictures that appeared in the press. The ones the prosecutors used to argue that I posed an imminent threat to the community: the ones where I had a gag in my mouth and arm and leg manacles. The expression on my face was a grimace of pain from having my shoulder wrenched, and the two officers carrying me were clearly acting for the photographer that they had arranged to be there.

It's only a twenty-minute flight to Juneau. The three of us took up the back row of the plane, and they finally cuffed me in front once there were no more good photo ops. It was rough as the jet blustered through ten thousand feet and bounced through the storm winds east to the state capital. All that met us at the airport was a local cop car, and we were at the intake gate of Lemon Creek Correctional Center, before my boys in the Sitka jail were eating their Salisbury steak and cold potatoes.

Lemon Creek is a prison. Some inmates are there serving out their long felony sentences, and there are inmates serving their three days for drunk driving.

Everyone is admitted and then they sit in a holding cell while they are processed and classified as to their security level. Some may move to a halfway house outside the razor wire, and some may leave holding for the bowels of protective segregation. Realistically it should take two hours to be processed, but it may take three days.

Understand, Your Honors, prison is an authoritarian regime in which the rules change every day, every hour sometimes. This is intended to make it hard for the inmates to plan any shenanigans, but it is also difficult on the employees. In a real prison, as opposed to a local jail, the jailers are not glad to see you, and all the bullshit that comes into the institution on your coattails is just more bullshit that they have to stutter-step their way through until the end of their shift. The fact that I had been with the Public Defender Agency and had already received death threats from some of my former clients was just a big pile of ongoing shit the guards had to deal with.

I spent seven days in holding. There was talk about putting me directly into Seg, but apparently there was some blowback on that plan. There was talk about keeping me in medical, although I was feeling much better, and I was cleared by my Sitka doc to have antibiotics administered if I started running a fever. The clearance in my file was key to my survival inside. Evidently there was some argument as to how much the State of Alaska wanted me protected.

Holding is a fish tank: they watch you on camera or actual "eyes on" twenty-four seven. They watch to see if you are slipping drugs out of your ass. Some inmates have to shit in a bucket, and a guard has to go through it. This does not make for happy relationships. They watch for self-destructive behavior, or for life-threatening behavior. If you have detox problems or if you are "a picker" like some of the methamphetamine addicts, they might put you in a "Gumby suit," which is much like a neoprene marine survival suit except you are locked into it, so you can't use your fingers or hit your head directly against the solid walls, which is a common injury in holding. Some people knock their heads against the walls out of genuine suicidal anxiety, some do it to fake injuries at the hands of the guards, which is another cause for disgruntlement among the staff, so much so that all acts of self-harm come to be treated as another form of disobedience.

On the seventh day, I was released into population and walked down to G dorm through a series of locked gates and concrete brick hallways. The hallway running past the central staircase had a gate approximately every thirty feet, and at each gate my escort stopped and waited to be buzzed through by Control. At each gate we waited for differing amounts of time. Twice the guard clicked the radio mic at his shoulder and gave the number to be opened. Still nothing happened, where the next gate would mysteriously open immediately. The first time you go through this, you think someone is messing with you. Do it a few more times and you realize you have no control of your movement and surrender your will to distant and capricious fate. Which is the point.

Finally, a long hallway appeared, and we were walking quickly. I was carrying a new set of sheets and a change of orange scrubs. A bell rang and doors buzzed open, and the hallway filled with men in either orange, green or red scrubs. Native men with buzzcuts and ponytails, black men with cornrows, white men with arms covered in tattoos, old men slumping along close to the wall trying to disappear, and young bodybuilders taking up half the hallway. I kept my eyes to the front and in the middle distance. I made no eye contact and held my linens out a bit from my body. As we walked past a corner in the hall, I eased to the side to follow the guard, who took two steps ahead of me to clear a path. Something slammed into me from the side, a shoulder, a forearm, near the exit wound, and I sprawled on the floor. Suddenly it was quiet and all I heard was the sound of boots on linoleum: men hurrying to get out the next door or through the next gate.

My escort turned back and saw me. Saw blood on the outside of my clean scrubs.

The guard said something into his radio, and all the thick deadbolts within my hearing slid shut. "Everyone grab some floor. Asses down, hands on heads. Now, God damn it." His voice echoed along the walls.

There were only six men in our rectangle of hallway by the time I rolled over. Their fingers were laced together on top of their heads. Their eyes staring at the floor.

The guard touched the damp blood on my shirt. "Gosh darn it, Younger, did you get stabbed already?"

"No." I said. "It's old." I stood up.

"Then what the hell happened?"

"I stumbled," I said. "I'm sorry."

"Well what do you think, you need medical?"

"No. I'm fine. I'll just put something on it. It's not bad."

"Good. Now get back down on the floor. We're locked down, asshole. I don't know when they are going to let us move." Two white men on the floor with long hair down the sides of their faces tried to stifle laughter.

It was close to his lunchtime and he didn't need this, my escort explained. I grabbed some floor and waited the twenty or so minutes until someone inexplicably opened the next gate.

G dorm was next to an outer wall by a door. Through the door, outside in what had once been a garden plot, were several tents for housing the overflow inmates. The prison was designed for four hundred, and there were close to nine hundred locked in now. There were lots of "pre-trials" housed in overflow. Some chose sleeping on the floor rather than the tents. I was led to the inside dorm and assigned a bottom bunk. There was a pillow by the wall and a thin mattress rolled up on the metal slab. The guard put me on the bed and told me to stay, then he walked around a corner out of sight and came back with a small stack of cheap paper towels that had come from a dispenser.

"Don't get blood on your towels or linens. You'll get written up," he said and threw them down on my bunk. "Get somebody else to show you the ropes. I'm going to lunch while I still can." He turned and walked down the row of bunks as his radio hissed. Then, just before he got to the gate, he turned and said, "Mind your own business in here, Younger. Just do easy time. Ya know what I'm saying?"

I nodded, and he was gone. Heads turned toward me from the bunks, heads appeared from the top bunks. Familiar faces and strangers alike.

"No way!" someone called out. "My lawyer's bitch is in jail? No way!"

I stood up and heard the scuffling of shoes, someone coming toward me. I felt a hand on my shoulder, sucked in my breath and turned with my fist raised.

"Cecil!" Gudger called out holding his hands out and putting both of them on my shoulders. "Cecil, it's me."

Catcalls came from down the row of bunks. Whistling and insults. Laughter and comments about the quality of their representation. "The Pretender is in the house. This is an opportunity we can't pass up," just about summed up the general consensus.

"What are you doing here?" I asked him.

"I don't know man. They just picked me up. I took the ferry to Juneau, and at my first meal at the shelter the cops picked me up."

"But what are the charges?"

"I don't know, Cecil."

"What do you mean you don't know? You must have some paperwork."

"I didn't keep it. You know . . . I had been . . . partying."

"Call David. He will help you."

"Cecil!" Now Gudger's eyes were wide with excitement. "There is some deal where Mr. Ryder can't be my lawyer because of that . . . thing we did with the building and the water." He was smiling at me with a strangely gleeful expression. "At least that's what I think. He won't talk with me. I've got some contract lawyer, I guess."

"Have you called them?"

"Man, I'm fine. I'm out of the rain. I couldn't get dry out there."

"What about Boomer?" I asked.

"He's down in D dorm. I saw him at the library. He's pretrial but I'm not sure for what. We will see him later, I suspect. Come on."

Gudger led me by the shoulder toward the shower area, which people appeared to be using for privacy on a first-come-first-serve basis. When we rounded the corner, there were two inmates standing very close together appearing as if they had just backed away from a kiss. They looked at Gudger and scuffled out without comment.

"I need to talk with you, Cecil. Listen, your man is here."

"My man?" I turned and stared at the two men walking away from us.

"Sanders," he whispered. "He's talking some ignorant shit in here."

"What kind of ignorant shit?"

Gudger looked around, clearly not wanting to be overheard. Out in the dorm there was an argument brewing about what TV show to watch. "He's talking about offering a lot of money to the guy who takes you down."

"Takes me down?"

"As in kills you. But there are very few guys in here doing a whole day who would be willing to draw that much heat, and the ones who might be willing are old as fuck . . . as old as you, man."

I looked around, the argument was getting louder. "A whole day?"

"All day . . . life in prison." He looked back into the dorm. "Hold on a second . . ." Gudger strode out like a junior-high homeroom teacher and told the two men who were arguing to sit down and be quiet. Then he gave a small Native-looking boy the chair closest to the TV and told him to choose. He looked around at the group of eight men to see if there was going to be any more to the argument. They said nothing and Gudger walked back to me.

Your Honors, I knew Gudger as a homeless inebriate, I thought of him as barely clinging to life, but here he was clean and bright and apparently in charge.

"Gudge, you look good man . . . What's the deal?"

"Cecil, it takes a week or so for all the alcohol to

burn out of my body, you know, to get rid of the cramps and the shaking. But after that I'm pretty good."

"Besides that, these guys listen to you. Are you some kind of badass?" We walked back to his office area.

He shook his head with a melancholy pride. "Naw . . . I just been in jail a lot. This is a medium-security unit. The young guys are scared, and the old guys are just doing their time. I help 'em all out with how to stay safe. They call me the Crossing Guard in here. I keep the young ones out of trouble by schooling them up. You know, man, I've been in jail a lot." He leaned his head against the wall as if he were a tired parent getting a break while his kids watched cartoons.

"The POs say I'm 'institutionalized.'"

"You think that's true, Gudge?" I stood on the shower-room side of him so that anyone would have to get past him to get to me.

"You seen how I live, man. My life is shit. If 'institutionalized' means getting clean and warm and fed regularly for a few months a year, then . . . I guess I am."

I thought about this for a while. "How dangerous is it in here?"

"This unit is fine. Like I said we got mostly old guys and young guys on sex charges who are scared shitless someone's going to find out what they are here for. Chesters you know. Chester the Molester?"

"But they are not dangerous?"

"Naw . . . man . . . they're pussies . . . unless they get

really scared, then who knows? Some of them go off
the rails. But think about it, Cecil, these guys have
sex with children because they don't have the balls to
deal with a real woman, or to deal with the fact that
they really want to have sex with men They are not
naturally aggressive, they are just violent when they
think they have been found out."

He was still whispering, but now he leaned in closer.
"But you can't stay in the dorm with all of us all the
time. You will have to go to some programs, you'll have
to go to chow, the law library, the gym, or outdoor rec.
That's where you might meet some assholes, you know
what I'm saying?"

"But you said there weren't many guys who would
really hurt me."

"Yeah . . . I did." He shifted on his feet a little like
a boxer. "But you ever been bitten by a young dog?"

"Once," I said, honestly trying to remember.

"You think that dog was really mean?"

"What are you saying, Gudge?"

"Dogs bite mostly because they are scared, Cecil.
Some guy might stab you just to show the others not
to mess with him. These guys down here aren't real
gangbangers. They're wannabes. There's not a single
contract killer in this place right now. Every once in a
while, there might be some genuine American badass,
someone from down south who got scooped up here,
but this tank is pretty mellow. But you got to worry about
these ignorant wannabes. They are like two-hundred-
pound puppies: no judgment and sharp teeth."

"I know for a fact that Sanders isn't a puppy, Gudge."

"True that. But he has been running his mouth so much, I doubt the COs are going to let him anywhere near you. Besides, he is still pre-trial. There are cameras everywhere here. There are a few dangerous blank spots, where the cameras can't see. Low and in some corners: behind a shelf, then in most of the showers and cans. Those cameras make good evidence, Cecil. But even what the cameras can't see, there is almost always someone else around watching. Someone who would be happy to testify truthfully for some consideration of their own. This jail is a bad place to commit a murder."

"But for money, or like you say, out of fear?"

Gudger looked at me with a sober intensity I did not recognize in him before this very moment. He sounded different in prison. He held himself differently in prison. He was not homeless in prison. "Cecil, I had never heard of this fucking guy Sanders before he wanted to kill you, and he's from the town I grew up in. He is new on the scene, and he doesn't throw that much weight around. Most of these guys think he is a bullshitter."

"So, what do I do?"

"If you want to do easy time, which is what I do, avoid the blank spots, which I will show you, and don't say nothing about Sanders. You don't know him, you don't know what any of this shit is about. Don't talk about your case, don't go anywhere without a friend and avoid drama like the plague."

"Is there any other option?"

"You could kill him first."

"Wait a minute, Gudger, what did you just get done telling me?"

"There are always ways, Cecil."

"Shit, you are a badass." I stared at him with a new kind of amazement.

I mention this to you, Your Honors because most people in the straight world overlook the homeless. They are becoming invisible in our communities. Everything we do for them in terms of shelters and food and medicine—which I am all in favor of by the way—has a hidden priority. That is, to make them go away, to divert them into various treatment facilities, sort of holding pens to their natural habitat, which in America now is jail. I spent time on Gudger in this allocution because he is my friend, and he had surprising abilities to keep me alive, which I don't think can be denied, or used against me. For even if we create these new lawless jungles by the dozens, we cannot deny our responsibility for what comes out of them. Habitat shapes life, Your Honors, in a tide pool or a prison yard. Gudger should not be condemned for how you created him, and I am using up this extraordinary amount of time by arguing that I should not be either.

That first night in Lemon Creek, I lay in my bunk listening to the sound of men snoring, calling out in their sleep, and others yelling "shut up." One boy was crying uncontrollably while an old man on a bottom bunk close to me vigorously masturbated. I didn't sleep until I lost track of myself and sleep rescued me.

Gudger helped me navigate the chow line in the mess hall and explained the importance of the seating arrangements. There is a line in that winds through the food service and then out, cafeteria style. The black gang members sit in the tables nearest the exit from the line. Violent white inmates sit at the tables near the entrance, and behind them older white offenders trying to keep a low profile. Natives—southeastern Tlingits, and northern Yupik or Inupiats who are not high-profile sex offenders sit in the middle behind the blacks. Asians, Filipinos and Pacific Islanders, of whom a disproportionately high number are Tongan, sit behind the whites by the entrance. Toward the exit side are hard-time white guys—gang members, white supremacists, and some of the more racist Christians. In the back, by the door where there are usually more guards, sit the known sex offenders, who are ostracized by everyone.

Usually there is a high-status inmate at the center of each population: a leading gangbanger, a head Native, the chief bull-goose crazy white nationalist, and so on. The farther away you sit from the head guy, the less influence he exerts over you. Gudger sat on the edge of the Native section by the Pacific Islanders. He looked around the chow hall and people gave him deference. He sat me with him and others at the table made room for me without question.

It was here that Gudger warned me about the

locations of the blank spots on the surveillance camera setup. These are the places of danger, Your Honors, I told you about the seating arrangement because the Prosecution has intimated that Gudger was a gang leader, and he was part of the conspiracy. But the affiliation of the men at this table was a product not of some criminal conspiracy but by the jail culture you yourselves have a part in creating. Jail is the largest growing institution in America. I am sorry to be taking up Your Honors' valuable time, but I am trying to give you the context of the evidence and the testimony that came before you.

A tray slammed down hard on the table next to me. Robert Boomer lurched onto the bench. "What up, Cecil? What you doing sitting with the fucking Indians?" He looked at Gudger.

I winced. "What the hell, Boomer?"

Boomer ducked his head, and whispered. "Jesus, Cecil . . . I'm in a dorm with a bunch of crazy-ass white guys. They will break my head open if I fraternize."

I stared at him. I tried to think of how much I didn't really know about the bomb-making Robert Boomer.

"Gudger knows what I'm talking about." He stared hard at my protector as if he were both mad and pleading.

Gudger nodded at both of us. "It's true. His dorm is shit. Part of the ivory trade. They break bones."

"Dude, law library. Later." Then Boomer stood up as if angry. "See you fucking blubber eaters later," and he took his tray away.

"Blubber eater?" I looked at Gudge.

"I have no idea, Cecil, I think he just made that up."

After breakfast on the first morning, we went to the law library, Gudger showed me around the stacks. As I walked in there was a young white man working at the front desk. He had thick glasses in black square frames and a pencil behind his ear. He looked to be checking in books. His shirt was tucked in very neatly. He wore green scrubs, which indicated he was in medium security, general population. Red scrubs indicated higher security risks or a prisoner straight out of segregation. The thin librarian offered to show me around the library and how to Shepardize a case, getting all the related cases for a particular legal question. I looked at Gudger, and he nodded in approval as I walked back in the stacks with the librarian.

The skinny librarian was unenthusiastically showing me the books and the process when he stopped and whispered, "You're some kind of lawyer, right?"

"No, I'm . . . was . . . an investigator," I told him in my normal tone.

"But you worked for David the nigger lawyer, right?"

"Yes . . . sorry, black . . . but as an investigator."

"Can you get him to write me an evidentiary motion on my case? I done all the research. I can give it to you." He looked at me as if he were scared shitless. "Here, come back here. I've got it squirreled away back here." He started walking toward the corner. The law library looked like a small well-scrubbed library in some threadbare technical college, with very thick walls and small unbreakable windows. Once we got there I noticed that the kid looked pale and his hands were shaking.

"I'm not feeling so great, I'm sorry but can you reach my folder there on the top shelf?" he asked me in almost a whisper.

It was as I reached for the folder, which was high enough that I had to stand on my toes and stretch myself up and off balance, that it dawned on me that I had made a mistake.

He reached in his shirt, then jerked out something I didn't recognize. His shirt buttons popped off, I saw that clearly, just before he slashed me. It drew little blood, and I came down on his head with my elbow and tried to grab his wrist. He lunged at me once more, and we fell against the stacks, knocking books to the floor.

Then Gudger was there with Boomer. Quietly and quickly they wrestled the librarian to the ground. They pummeled him on his body so as to leave no bruises his clothes wouldn't cover. Boomer swung a big blue statute book over his head and smacked the kid in the face hard enough to make a popping sound. They subdued him in less than twenty seconds. No blood was flowing, but the kid's face was bright red and bore a grimace of pain. Then they jerked him to his feet, and pushed him toward his desk. They said nothing, no swearing or threats. Just like that . . . it was as if nothing had happened. There was nothing incriminating said or much of anything observable. All that was left were the kid's injuries, and a memory he would not want to use for fear of getting another beating.

I stood there holding his elaborate shiv in my hand. It had been made of a handful of #2 pencils with razor blades from small disposable razors inserted into the blunt ends. The whole bundle was expertly held together with black-tarred twine. The whipping on the pencils looked to have been made by someone who knew nautical knots and was of the best quality. The blades formed a kind of razor flower on the end and came to a point that would be deadly if you dug down to hit an artery. The librarian had wanted to slice my femoral artery, but he only scratched my stomach.

"Thanks," I said to my friends.

"Man, you are a shitty jail friend." Gudger smiled at me, and Boomer, who laughed, high-fived him as we walked out.

I looked at the scratches on my stomach. "What was that? You think he wanted Sanders's reward?"

Boomer watched me with a look of concern. "Was he one of your clients?" he asked.

"What are you saying? All my clients want to kill me?"

"I'm just saying, dude." Boomer shrugged.

"What do you know about Sanders?" I asked the bomb maker.

"The guy is out of his mind. He runs his mouth all day long about his crazy shit politics and racist crap. It's irritating. Half the guys in the dorm want to kill him and the other half believes his promises to make them rich. Rich . . . Jesus H. Christ on a crutch . . .

I'd pay more than he could afford just to get away from him."

"Did Sanders himself say anything about wanting to kill me, Boomer?"

Boomer stopped in the hall and looked at me as if I were joking, "Dude. Of course he wants to kill you. He's always wanted to kill you. What movie have you been watching?"

"Thanks, Boomer," I said, probably more sarcastically than I meant to. "Did he give you any specifics? Anything I could use to be prepared?"

"It's not like we have workshops, Cecil. We don't break out into small groups and write on easels and shit. No, I don't know plans."

"I'm glad you are amused."

"Fuck off. I'm in jail too, you know."

"Right. I'm sorry."

Gudger stood in front of us and whispered, "Can you two lovebirds save this discussion for another place?"

"What? What did I say?" Boomer looked at us genuinely confused.

"Never mind," I told him, and we walked down the clattering hall of jail-meat shoving up against the next gate.

The next three days went on uneventfully. I took some elbows in the gut walking in the halls. There were catcalls and whistles, insults by the score: references to my mother, references to my sexual preference, unprovoked evaluations of my talents as an investigator and a man who passed on advice to defendants. It was a field day for the insult comics behind bars. The best one was a guy who came up to me and parroted back my own words to him by saying in a childish singsong voice, "Remember, it's bad now, but it could always get worse if you talk about your case." Then he just stood there and stared at me with an angry and sad expression and added, "It gets worse anyway, doesn't it, fuckwad?"

I have considered working on a new jailhouse edition of *Baby's First Felony,* but this one would be written in the form of *Miss Manners*: *When making wine in your toilet, be sure to scrub the john carefully, and be sure to have enough cups for everyone.*

Gudger stayed in my orbit and kept watch. A couple of pedophiles I knew stayed very close to me, sometimes reading over my shoulder and turning the pages of my book. They tried to be nice but were unable to control their unremitting obsequious manners. They didn't want to have sex with me because I was way too old, but the most irritating thing about pedophiles is that they have spent most of their lives manipulating everyone around to prevent them from discovering their horrible secret. This effort has consumed them to such an extent that even when their secret has been told to the entire world they cannot help but keep up the full-court press of trying to convince everyone that they are just one of the guys . . . by standing too close and being uncomfortably familiar . . . which really dosen't work in jail.

"Give us some fucking space . . ." Gudger said with some authority and shooed them off my bunk like bugs.

I ate every day with Gudger's guys, who were mostly alcoholics and drug addicts. There were also a few tough boys with broad, flat fists and tear drops tattooed on their cheeks to mark the time they had done. I felt myself falling into the rhythm of being caged, squirreling my shiv in a lose piece of ceiling tile, harboring my secrets among my own set of friends. Every day some old client would come forward and try to talk with me in a friendly way, but I never knew if they were helpful or planning to cut out my liver. I kept my distance. I was slowly becoming a convict.

On the third week, I was lying in my bunk reading an outdoor magazine that Gudger had lent me, and I looked up and saw Trooper Brown walking past the door of the unit. He was with three other prison officials. They stopped and walked in our dorm, and we all stood up, thinking the dorm was going to be tossed for contraband. The ceiling tile holding the shiv was nowhere near my bunk, but I suddenly remembered I hadn't wiped it down for prints.

Brown looked right through me when his eyes scanned the room. He gave no impression that he had seen or recognized me. He walked around the dorm while the prison officials talked to several inmates, including Gudger. I could not hear the conversation. Then they called three of them to the law library. Brown went with them and stayed in the hall for perhaps ten or fifteen minutes. When they came back in, Gudger walked past me to his bunk giving me a shrug like he didn't know what they were up to. Then the main prison official, later identified to me as the assistant superintendent, cleared his throat and announced that our shower room was going to be closed for the rest of the day and night while they did some work on the plumbing, and he gave us instructions about where and when we would be able to shower during that time. They taped off the shower room and posted a guard in the dorm. Then all of them left, including Brown.

"They asked about the law library, but I told them it was just an argument and nothing happened that would cause a write up," Gudger whispered to me as we were all mopping the floor of the dorm after they were gone. "They don't know shit. The punk must have said something to somebody. Or maybe somebody saw his bruises and wrote a cop-out." A cop-out was a written request to speak to someone in administration.

I said nothing more about it. It would be bad for the guard to see the group of us from the law library talking together. But later that night, I retrieved the shiv and put it in my pillowcase. Gudger had helped me fashion a cap for the blades out of an old pill bottle. It slipped neatly over the razor tip and we were able to secure it with a small lanyard made from a section of shoelace. Prison is a hive of little craft projects like that.

Under the watchful eye of some guards, plumbers

came into our shower room and banged around on pipes. They carried their tools in prison-approved soft bags, bringing only the necessary tools in and making sure there was a strict accounting for each tool when they left the shower room. Nothing could be left for the inmates to use for their illicit crafts. Besides weapons, almost everyone worked on something: stills to ferment fruit smuggled back from chow, packets to be given to relatives to smuggle drugs back in, pipes to smoke the drugs. Some inmates even liked to fashion exotic sex toys for their newfound enjoyment of gay sex.

Two days after the plumbers left G dorm, a CO came in the morning and called out a change of schedule. He read off names and some they sent to programs like alcohol or anger management. Some they called out for medical, and some they called out for visiting. When he got done calling them all out there was only me, Gudger, and two others left in the dorm for the day. Then he announced that the four of us would be locked down without food. There was no discussion. No explanation. Gudger tried to ask questions, but the CO was having none of it. All he told Gudger was, "I'm the messenger. You want to discuss it, you can write a cop-out and take it up with the superintendent." Which was hardly an offer because none of us would be able to write such a request while we were locked down, and then it would be days, perhaps weeks before we might get an answer just on our request to talk to someone in admin about the lockdown.

Gudger didn't push it. The dorm cleared out and we were alone. We sat at the far end and started a game of poker using round crackers for chips. One of the buddies was cleaning up at the game but was eating his winnings almost as fast as he won. Three hours went by as we enjoyed the relative quiet and security of being by ourselves.

Then the far door opened and a guard walked in. Just in front of him was Wynn Sanders, smirking and rolling his shoulder, as if he were a street brawler.

My stomach tightened but I kept dealing. I had called five-card stud, jacks or better to open with a progressive ante. Nothing wild.

"You want in?" I called over my shoulder to Sanders.

"Well, hello boys, what are the stakes?" he said.

"Crackers, I'll stake you."

"Keep your crackers, Mr. Younger," he said sweetly.

Gudger smiled at Sanders as he walked up to the table. "Well that's unfriendly."

"You in a bad mood bro?" The buddy who was eating his winnings also smiled and leaned over his stack and flexed his rather sizeable biceps.

"You boys play nice," the CO called from the end of the dorm. "I don't want any complaints or problems out of you little rascals."

"Yes, dear," the other buddy sang out while he stared hard at Sanders. "You heard the man."

"You boys and your endless games," Sanders said, and I was getting the idea that Sanders, while actually a monster, was also a coward, trying desperately to act tough. I was betting now that he was scared shitless of being in jail with all the "mud people" he so despised.

"An eighty-eight?" Gudger nodded toward Sanders's tattoo on the back of his wrist. "Now that's *so* scary." He smirked.

"What's the eighty-eight about?" I asked.

"Oh, Jesus, it's their little secret code sort of thing. It's pathetic." Gudger spoke loud enough to make sure Sanders could hear.

"Whose little code?" I asked, keeping my voice loud as well.

"It started in a California jail. Eight is for the eighth letter in the alphabet, *H*, and in some of the earliest prison code writing *H* stands for Heil Hitler. It's juvenile."

Sanders flopped down on a bunk that was four down from mine on the bottom. A convict who had been moved home for court had vacated this bunk, where now Sanders rubbed his dirty socks on his own pillow.

"How can you eat those nasty crackers?" Sanders muttered toward the card table.

The buddy put down his cards. "Yo, that reminds me of a story. This little boy was sitting down on the beach unwrapping and eating maybe a dozen chocolate bars, and an old man comes up to him and says, 'You know, you shouldn't eat so much chocolate. That stuff is bad for you.' The little boy looks up at the old man from the rock he is sitting on and says, 'I don't know about that. My grandfather lived to be a hundred and six years old,' and the old man looks down

and says, 'Oh, I'm so sorry. Did he eat a lot of chocolate?' and the little boy says, 'No, but he learned to
mind his own fucking business.'"

The four of us laughed out loud, long and hard, the
three mud people and me, while Sanders scowled in
his bunk, unable to laugh, which made me particularly
happy because I hated to think of that excellent joke
traveling so far and so fast to land on his tone-deaf
ears. In my experience, racists never appreciate either
folklore or a good joke.

As the programs ended and guys came out of holding blocks, other inmates starting filing back to the
dorm: Native guys and black men, Hispanics and
Tongans. It was a loud roughhouse gang of people
from all over the world. One of the older Filipino men
brought us corn bread from lunch and another Native
guy brought us cartons of milk. No one spoke with
Sanders, a couple of the white kids looked him up and
down as they passed but walked quickly by without a
word. One of them broke out a plastic bear of honey
and let us eat it on our corn bread. The night wore on
with quiet television and conversation. An old man
sang songs in Spanish. The songs sounded melancholy
to our ears, and the mood was calm for the first time
during my time in jail. The cards flopped down softly
on the table, and dominos rattled away on a bunk without its mattress, while players did pushups, awaiting
their turn to play.

All during the evening Sanders harbored his dying
privilege to himself while rage burned behind his eyes.

He spoke to no one. He had nothing to read and he couldn't borrow or bully anyone for a favor. He was alone in a country not his own. Soon the lights went out, and the noises turned to the nocturnal breathing of men alone in their own thoughts.

The next morning the CO came back and read off a list of names again. This time he read everyone's name but Sanders's and mine. Then he explained that Sanders and I were to go to morning meal after cleanup and come back to the dorm for lockdown. I looked at Gudger and he shook his head, warning me not to say anything to the CO. We cleaned the dorm and while we mopped, Gudger whispered, "I don't know what this is about. Go to the can on the way to chow. Don't go in the shower room or the can at any time you are in here with him alone." I nodded.

I asked the CO in the mess hall if I could take some cold pancakes back to the dorm for lockdown, and he nodded and waved me out into the hall. I used the can near the booking area. Sanders was nowhere in sight. I walked slowly down the halls and rushed through the locking doors to make sure I wasn't in a blocked section with him. As I approached G dorm I saw the plumbers again coming out with their canvas bags. One of them looked at me and then looked away quickly. When I walked through the door into our dorm, the hall was empty. The bunk beds looked like rows of empty bookshelves. The TV was off, and the floor was slick and clean with a new coat of wax that a con had buffed up during chow.

Fluorescent lights buzzed on their dangling cords from the ceiling. Wynn Sanders was sitting at the card table playing a game of solitaire, staring intently at his cards. A buzzer sounded, then the doors swung shut and locked.

I walked to my bunk and plumped up my pillow.

"Don't get comfortable, Mr. Younger," Sanders said to me. "We have business to conduct."

"No, we don't."

"Boy, now let me try my carrots before I get to my sticks. I have money. How much would it take for you to keep your mouth shut?"

"You killed Thistle . . . two girls actually. You killed them both, Bean and Thistle." My voice broke while it built with rage. "You killed Thistle, then you cut her foot off and delivered it to my home, just to torment my wife. Shit. A brown bear boar will eat a cub but . . . but, that's somehow . . . in it's nature . . . I'm sure there is some logic . . . some fucking bear logic to it. You have no nature at all." I sat on my bunk holding my pillow on my lap now.

"I needed something to put pressure on you, Cecil. You are so soft-hearted I knew it wouldn't take much. Remember, I didn't kill either of them. Sweeper disposed of the first girl after she died of an overdose, and, well, you saw how he killed that friend of your daughter's. And Cecil"—here he lowered his voice and pointed at me—"I didn't cut her foot off. I just picked it up off the table when Sweeper was processing her for disposal. Listen, when you think about it, I did you a favor when I killed him." He kept looking at the cards, flipping one off the top of the deck and looking at it for a long time before putting it in place.

"What about the Mexican Mule and his backup in the car?"

"Now that's true. I'm sorry I left them out. That was another public service I performed. We don't need foreign companies doing business in Alaska. Not when we can do it ourselves. I finally had to do the man you refer to as the mule, and, of course, Sweeper was the lookout. Sweeper was particularly bloodthirsty. He had been on the pipe a long time, and it was eating his brain up. He was good, cheap labor. I just paid him in product and promises. He was very compliant . . . until he wasn't, of course."

"What did you mean 'finally had to do' the mule?" I asked him.

"Oh . . . the lieutenant was supposed to take care of that. I provided law enforcement with all the information. But . . . well, you know how it is better than anyone. They didn't move on him. They futzed around, and finally the timing was perfect and I had to step in."

"The lieutenant was going to kill him for you?"

Sanders chuckled a bit as he placed a new king on the top row. "Well, you know, obviously I would have preferred that. I mean, who is really going to care about a Mexican drug dealer? No trial and testimony and all that. I could have been happy with an arrest. But the police are so hidebound by rules and procedure. Government stuff. It was taking forever. I owned the poor lieutenant, and I thought I had him sewn up. But he took the coward's way out when I demanded that he take care of Sherrie Gault."

"Yeah . . . what about Sherrie? What about her? She's a loose end, isn't she?"

"Oh my Lord, no, Cecil. She took carrots. She took carrots: my business interest in Mexico, Southern California and the Sweeper's body in exchange for loyalty. She is a lot meaner than she looks. Sweeper was a bad boyfriend. Apparently, she was tired of having her jaw broken."

"Yeah . . . I was always rooting for Sherrie to dump his ass," I said as Sanders threw down the cards.

"That leaves you my friend. You really are the last one standing."

We looked at each other across the ten-foot stretch from my bunk to the iron table with the fixed seats.

"Wait a minute . . . back up. Did the lieutenant really have sex with those young girls? That's how you owned him, right?"

"Now . . . that's a funny story, that." Sanders had a tight, cold smile. "He thought he slept with them. The lieutenant was a big old slab of American beef, you know what I'm saying? He liked to laugh and to gamble and to drink. He told bad jokes and he was, I don't know . . . kind of whimsical. Late at night he couldn't control his appetites. He drank too much and he laughed too hard, and he didn't really look carefully at the girls I brought in. But I didn't pimp those girls to him. I'm crass, son, but I'm not sick. Late one night he woke up with a hell of a hangover and two naked girls draped over him. I drugged the girls, so they weren't aware of anything. You needn't worry."

"I'm so relieved," I said as I worked my shiv up the sleeve of my right arm.

"Well, anywho, with a few choice words from the girls and Sweeper and me, he fully believed he had had . . . congress with them."

Sanders looked out the thin windows out onto the abandoned garden plots in the yard where the tomato strings and sticks lay helter-skelter in the mud. Rain dotted the puddles and softened the mud to rivulets.

"And, boy I tell you, he was upset. He was worried about being unfaithful to his wife. I thought he was going to kill himself right then. Like I said, he was a regular guy. I didn't have the heart to tell him the girls were under the age of consent and the crime he believed he had committed was actually an unclassified felony with a nonnegotiable twenty-five-year term. No. I saved that until I really needed it. I thought that was my ace"— here he lifted up an ace of spades and waggled it at me—"in the hole. You know what I'm saying?"

"So, he really killed himself?" I said with more skepticism than I should have.

"Mr. Younger, I'm telling you he was a good, sensitive man. The God's honest truth. When I told him the girls' ages, and I asked him to do me the favor of killing Sherrie, he took out his pistol and shot himself in the mouth. Surprised the hell out of me. Tragic, really. I'm serious. He was a good, good man. Such a waste, particularly when I found out that little cunt could be bought so cheap."

I gripped the shiv in my right hand now. Covered by the pillow.

"All right then," Sanders continued, "let's sort this out. How much?"

"What?"

"How much for your loyalty. Your girl is going to need some medical expenses. Name a price."

"Can't do it."

"Come on, Cecil. We don't need to go through this trouble. Are you sure?"

"Well . . . let me think. Nope, I'm sure. You are a pimp and a cheap hustler, besides being a raving racist prick. There is not enough God damned money in the world for me to be indebted to you."

"Cecil, come on. Really. I'm not a pimp. I told you that. I didn't put those girls out to have sex with other men." Here he stared at me calmly. "I saved them for myself."

Your Honors, I'm here to tell you today that my vision darkened, and I took that shiv out from under my pillow and stood up, every inch of my body shaking.

"Yeah boy. This is how it's going to go." He spit his words at me. "You are going to take that shiv that I made sure you got from that faggot in the library, and you are going to lunge at me, then I'm going to kill you. Right here on camera."

"You. Stop talking. Now." I managed to say those words.

"I'm not going to stop talking, I had wonderful sex with your little girl. What are you going to do, Mr. Younger? You're a government worker. You never really do, anything, do you? You are a joke."

"Come into the shower room," I said, and walked away from him.

The shower room floor was slick. I was looking down a red tunnel of light.

He came around the corner. "You are pathetic. This is still going to go down the way I said. I'll just have to fake an injury to get self-defense. But Cecil, I *am* going to kill you." he said.

"No," I said, and then I said the most damning words a man could say. "No sir, I intend to kill you first." I said it, Your Honors. I fully admit it. Then he took a step toward me and reached into his pants and pulled out a piece of iron bar that had been sharpened to a shiny point. He lunged at me but slipped on the floor just a bit. I stepped back and kicked him hard on the side of his knee and he collapsed. I then pulled his hair back so that his white neck was exposed to the flimsy light in the shower room. He stabbed me in the thigh with the iron bar. I could see his pulse fluttering on his neck. I looked at my unrecognizable face, contorted by pain in the reflection of one of his eyes. Then knowing full well what I was doing, I slit his throat.

His blood became a fountain. It pattered down on the tiles, swirled around the center drains and gurgled down the pipes. As his heartbeat slowed, the spray of blood weakened. My hands were crimson and greasy with blood. My pants and shirt were soaked through, and Wynn Sanders was soppy wet all down the front of his prison scrubs. When he slumped to the tile, I finally felt the pain in my leg where the shiny tip of the bar was buried in my femur. Much more quickly than I expected, the dorm was flooded with officers, including Trooper Ray Brown, who laid me down on the tile and wrapped some towels around my leg.

"It's all on tape . . ." I remember him saying as I lay shivering on the dark-red floor. "Take him first, get him to medical right now." Brown barked out the orders and two big men lifted me. "This man is the priority here."

Wynn Sanders's face lay bone white on the white tile floor, the slash I had made on his throat had stopped bubbling. His eyes were wide open with surprise, staring up at the white ceiling. As they carried me out, I imagined I saw a shimmering form rising up out of his body, and that form was black . . . the dense construction of every color in the spectrum. It rose up into the empty pale ceiling and was gone.

As you know, Your Honors, Trooper Brown had been conducting an investigation into my allegations ever since we had spoken at the hospital. He had secretly made the promise that he would do it with Wendy Sasserman so that I couldn't "jigger with his fact finding," as Ms. Sasserman put it. Trooper Brown had found the trace evidence of blood and hair of Melissa Bean in the sink traps and drain piping below

the meth lab. He had found blood evidence in the car-
peting of the floor of the hotel. Thankfully the mother
of the Mexican Mule had saved his wisdom teeth in her
hope chest and was able to provide a DNA match. The
counter man at the hotel was happy to share an account
of seeing his boss get a revolver out of the safe and
head upstairs after I had gone up to the room, and the
crew of Mexican workers at the fish plant were happy
to go home at the end of the season on the Immigra-
tion Services' dime after they fingered the two guys on
their crew who handled the disposal of the bodies for
Señor Sanders. They also provided gloves and knives
that retained bloodstain evidence. Apparently no one
cleans their stuff with hydrogen peroxide.

Finally, Trooper Brown had the shower room in G
dorm wired with cameras and sound after getting a tip
from a CO, who said Sanders had offered him a bribe
to get him transferred into G dorm and to get him
alone with me. Brown got all of that done, and luckily
the microphones were so sensitive and well-placed that
they picked up our conversation at the card table, but
as you know, Trooper Brown was not sure if Sanders
was intent on carrying through with actually killing me
or just trying to buy me off with the added motivation
of floridly violent threats. Or at least that is the reason
Trooper Brown gave in his testimony for not stepping
in sooner in the shower room.

Your Honors, there is a section of *Baby's First Felony*
that says, *Keep your allocution short, show remorse, take
responsibility and show you can do better. Never say or imply,*

"I didn't do it . . . but if I did, the son of a bitch deserved it." Which is frankly, in a very long-winded manner, exactly what I've done in my statement today. I have learned many things during this experience, and after eighteen months in jail now, during my investigation, trial, and sentence appeal, the most important thing I've learned, is that I have extraordinary potential to be rehabilitated. I cannot imagine this kind of thing happening to me ever again. The potential for me to commit this kind of crime again is exactly the criteria my lawyers are asking you to consider.

I come before you having been convicted of destruction of property, reckless endangerment, and involuntary manslaughter, by a jury of my peers. The jurors rejected my necessity defense, where I maintained I had no choice but to rescue my daughter in the manner I did. And they did not fully adopt my position of murder in the second degree, carried out in self-defense against Mr. Sanders. I also come before you having been convicted of felony DUI twice in my past, both counts I still maintain are outside the lookback period, but apparently, the laws recently changed. My minimum sentence for these charges is twenty-five to thirty-five years as per legislative mandate. My lawyer has argued that I pose an extraordinary possibility of reformation and that it would be "manifestly unjust" for me to serve such a long prison term. You have read the arguments, and I will let them stand for themselves.

Can I tell you I am some kind of exemplary person?

No, I don't think so. I have made colossal mistakes, and will make more I'm sure, but not of this nature. I am fifty-seven years old now, I would be some eighty years old if I were to receive the mandated minimum sentence, and honestly I cannot imagine another set of circumstances in which I would blow up an apartment house or kill an inmate in a prison cell if I were allowed to go home sooner than twenty-five years to be with my daughter, watch her graduate from high school, college, grow into a woman, and perhaps begin a family of her own.

Since my trial, Blossom has moved to Juneau. She goes to school there, and she lives on her mother's boat with her mom and her auntie. Every day that she is allowed, she comes to visit me, tells me jokes, and shows me her schoolwork. She calls me Daddy. Every time she gets up to go, and before she is put through the pat-down search, she tells me she loves me. She tells me that she will always love me and that she will come to the jail every day to see me.

Your Honors, I'm asking not only for my wife and me. I'm asking for Blossom, if you knew her you would know that she will do it. She will come every day to see me. She is stubborn that way. Please, please don't let her become a middle-aged woman visiting her father in jail and having to be subjected to pat-down searches every day from men who treat her like a convict herself. I will gladly submit to the cavity searches after each visit, but don't make her grow old coming to prison every day.

You have heard all this from every defendant who has come before you, and I am not asking to be seen as special or superior to any of those men. I am asking for your unique attention at just this moment. I am asking for your hard work, even though I may not be more deserving of it than others. I am asking that you use your intellect and observational skills to examine whether or not my case presents facts that could not have been predicted by our state legislators when they considered the cause of justice when passing the sentencing laws.

Your Honors, I mean no disrespect when I say that life shares the qualities of a good joke: it should be brief, well-chosen and end in surprise. Also in jokes, as in life, context is everything.

I know, we live in divisive times and although my case is odd and long, I am asking nothing more than any other citizen. There are men who will come before this bar long after I am gone who will have stories to tell, and, like them, I want to tell you that no matter the mistakes I have made, I am essentially, in my soul, a civilized man, and all I can offer for proof is that I love my daughter, and she loves me. For truthfully, Your Honors, if a man can love his daughter and she love him in return, with honesty and restraint, then what act, what station, can we aspire to . . . that would be more civilized than that?

Thank you for your patience, and I yield to my attorney.

PART TWO:

Memorandum of Decision by the
Three-Judge Sentencing Panel

IN THE SUPERIOR COURT FOR THE STATE OF ALASKA
FIRST JUDICIAL DISTRICT AT SITKA

STATE OF ALASKA)
)
Plaintiff)
)
vs.)
)
CECIL WAYNE YOUNGER,)
)
Defendant.)Case No. 11854
_____)

FINDINGS OF THE THREE-JUDGE PANEL
This Three-Judge Sentencing Panel held a hearing in this case. The parties appeared and were represented by their counsel of record with each side presenting evidence and argument. In

addition, the Panel has examined the pertinent files and records in this case, and in particular have reviewed the transcript of the trial. We have also heard what amounts to the longest allocution in the history of this Court.

The legislature has, by enacting Alaska Statute 12.55.175, created this three-judge panel to review extraordinary cases where the mandatory sentence, the presumptive sentence, would be manifestly unjust. The statute permits the court to sentence a defendant to less than that proscribed by the sentencing statutes if there are unusual mitigating circumstances.

In this case, we have been asked by the defendant to consider that the defendant has an exceptional potential for rehabilitation.

This Court finds that Mr. Younger's driving while intoxicated offenses are remote in time, and his current consumption of alcohol, in light of years of sobriety, was the result of extraordinary (quite possibly once-in-a-lifetime) circumstances. Any concern of relapse may be addressed in the conditions of probation.

Nor do we find that Mr. Younger presents a danger to the public.

We have relied, for our decision, on the extraordinarily favorable affidavit and testimony by Trooper Brown, and on Mr. Younger's statement to the court. We note that the state chose not to call their chief investigator to testify before this Court and has presented no evidence contrary to that asserted by Mr. Younger. We also find that despite his participation in the destruction of the Hillside Apartments, there is evidence that Mr. Younger tried to limit the danger to others. The Court also notes that he has no violent criminal history.

With respect to the charge of negligent homicide, this panel must take a restrained view and honor the jury's decision. We have no ability to overturn a conviction. However, in sentencing Mr. Younger, we shall take into account the significant weight of evidence in favor of self-defense and the necessity for his actions.

In formulating a sentence for Mr. Younger, we are struck by the unusual character of his offenses and know of no other case of a similar nature. The facts presented here have no comparisons in case law.

Based on the above, we therefore find that the defendant has an extraordinary potential for rehabilitation. It would be manifestly unjust to sentence Mr. Younger in the presumptive range, the minimum mandatory sentence of which is 25 years.

SENTENCE

The Panel imposes a sentence of six years to serve with no time suspended and a ten-year period of probation. Mr. Younger will be eligible for discretionary parole during the second half of his sentence.

CONDITIONS OF PROBATION

1) He is to complete all available drug/alcohol classes and anger-management classes while in confinement.

2) He is to report to his probation officer within two days of being released from jail.

3) He is to obey all laws and consume no alcohol (though he may be in establishments which sell or provide alcohol while he is working as an investigator, should he return to that profession).

4) He is to submit to random drug and alcohol testing conducted by the probation officer at his or her discretion.

5) He may not possess explosives nor apply for an explosives handler's license.

6) As a result of his felony conviction, he may not possess firearms or other weapons.

7) If he chooses to work as a private investigator, he be employed by a governmental agency under supervision of a member of the bar, an investigator with more than ten years of experience, or to carry a ten-million-dollar bond for damage and destruction.

8) He will follow all recommendations of his parole officer and the Department of Probation.

9) He will also attend parenting classes at the

discretion of the probation officer if for some reason, he fathers another child.

IT IS SO ORDERED.

Dated this day, in Anchorage, Alaska.

| Galen Pain | Jude Pate | Monica Eastham |

PART THREE:

Supplemental Evidence

Manual created by
David Ryder, Baby's First Felony

PART ONE:

FELONY: A crime of graver or more serious nature than those designated as misdemeanors. Under many state statutes, any offense punishable by death or imprisonment for a term exceeding one year.

So the prime directive when a crime is committed is:

Don't hurt the dog and don't do the meth.

Obeying the prime directive's twin goals of compassion and restraint should restrict most criminal endeavors to the misdemeanor level. The fact that you are consulting this manual means you have violated the prime directive!

Bruno's lawyer says:

"REMEMBER THE MOST IMPORTANT RULE!"

RULE #1

DON'T TALK TO THE COPS!!
ASK FOR YOUR LAWYER!!

PART TWo:

**While you are committing your first felony,
or immediately afterward . . .**

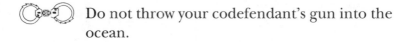

Do not throw your codefendant's gun into the ocean.

During field sobriety tests for your third drunk driving offense, do not tell the cops, "I can't even do this when I'm sober."

ASSAULTiNG BEHAViORS:

If someone calls you and wants to talk about the assault you committed against them the day before, the proper response is not, "Oh jeeze, I'm sorry. I'll never do it again."

If someone calls you and wants to talk about the assault you committed against them the day before, the proper response is, "I'm sorry, you are breaking up. I can't hear a word you are saying."

If someone calls you and wants to talk about the assault you committed against them the day before, they are sitting in the police station recording every word you are saying to them.

Bruno says:

SNACK-UMS GOOD!

Bruno's Lawyer says:

 Don't eat the cheese puffs when burglarizing a house. The yellow dust makes your fingerprints pop when the cops first arrive.

Don't eat the cheese puffs when burglarizing a house because the yellow dust all around your lips can be chemically linked to your fingerprints.

Other Good Ideas

iF PLANNING ON GETTING BLACK-OUT DRUNK . . .

LEAVE YOUR GUNS AT HOME.

When burglarizing your neighbor, do not step in dog poop before climbing through the window, then track the stuff all the way back to your bedroom.

When building a bomb, do not leave your to-do list with the words "buy a fuse" at the hardware store counter.

PART THREE

Bruno says:

"GAABA PIGGY BABBA SUCK IT!"

Bruno's Lawyer says:

Yes, talking is hard . . . so when you talk to the cops remember:

- Lick and stick this tattoo to the inside of your eyelids: "I don't want to talk to you without my lawyer."

- When you do talk with the cops, don't tell them that you didn't do it AND that the "asshole deserved it."

- **Explain or deny. Don't do both.**

- When talking about a female under 12 years old, do not refer to her as "that little bitch."

- When confessing to killing someone, do not use hunting analogies. "I've shot a lot of deer. I knew it was the right thing to put him out of his misery" is not going to help.

- Never use the phrase, "How dumb do you think I am?" You are just asking for an answer.

- Let's revisit, when the policeman says he just needs to ask you a few questions to "clear things up and get you on your way home," that officer is planning to keep you in jail for a long, long time.

- The first words out of your mouth are not, "Oh my God, is he dead?!" The first words out of your mouth are, "I really want to help you officer, but I really need to talk with my attorney."

PART FOUR:

**While you are
incarcerated
and awaiting trial:**

Do not take legal advice from a pedophile.

Do not take legal advice from anyone who has a sentence longer than three days.

Do not take legal advice from anyone with a sentence of less than four days.

The sign next to the jail phone saying your calls are being recorded is not being ironic.

When talking on the jail phone, Pig Latin is not an unbreakable code.

When talking on the jail phone, Spanish is not an unbreakable code.

Don't talk about your crimes on the jail phone in any language.

PART FIVE:

Dealing with your lawyer

Do not tell your public defender that your mother is sending you money for "a real lawyer" unless you have seen the check.

If you really want to get under your court appointed lawyer's skin, be original. The put-down "public pretender" is stale and tired. Try something new.

PART SIX:

Courtroom decorum and behavior

Do not wear the shoes you stole to court.

Make sure to turn off your cell phone or, even better, delete your current cell phone ringtone that says, "You get the drugs, I'll get the guns."

During allocution to the judge, keep it short, and don't tell the judge how much the victim deserved it.

AUTHOR'S NOTE

This is a work of fiction. In a sense it is a hallucinatory dream of everything that could have gone wrong for me while working thirty years as a criminal defense investigator in Alaska. Readers looking for clues to the underworld or the police work of the actual town of Sitka will be bitterly disappointed.

Much of the geography described is as you would find it in Sitka today, but there is no Hillside Apartment building and there never was one that I know of. You *can* get a cab ride from Hank Moore of Hank's Cab ("Honk if you have a ride, Hank if you don't"), but none of the lawyers, police officers or business people are remotely real. There are many poker games around town and there is a lot of gossip surrounding those games, but all the details I created in this story came from my imagination.

ACKNOWLEDGMENTS

My thanks go out to Finn Straley, who is a stand-up comedian in Los Angeles and has spent hours with me discussing the mechanics of jokes. It was from him that I learned to think about word selection, rhythm, context, folklore and the similarity to poetry. Thanks to Doug Comstock for his illustrations for the comic version of *Baby's First Felony*. Also thanks go to Marika Partridge and her son Chaney for their insight into humor therapy as it relates to autism. And to my friend Katrina Woolford, for her selection of truly heinous jokes, which always made me laugh.